The Dancer's Dilemma

by

Riley Blair

The Dancer's Dilemma

Cover Art by *Diana Carlile*

The Wild Rose Press, Inc.
PO Box 708
Adams Basin, NY 14410-0708
Visit us at www.thewildrosepress.com

Publishing History
First Champagne Rose Edition, 2019
Print ISBN 978-1-5092-2423-4
Digital ISBN 978-1-5092-2424-1

Published in the United States of America

Making a decision, she wrapped her arm around the back of his neck and pulled him toward her in a deep kiss. He gave in completely, stopping their bouncing progress and leaving water lapping around their entwined bodies.

It was a good kiss, that's for sure. She had kissed plenty of men, but none with this mix of passion and care. Under the water, his hand gently supported and caressed her lower back. She twisted the small tuft of hair at the back of his neck in response.

When the kiss finally ended, she wasn't sure who had pulled away first. They stayed suspended together, breathing heavily and running their fingers over each other's bodies.

"Bennett, I…" she began, but he silenced her with another kiss. She became weightless as he lifted her up by her hips, allowing her to wrap both legs around his waist as she hadn't done to a man since high school.

She sighed as he slid a hand up and under the back of her bikini top, gently loosening the strings. She was melting into his body with her hands still roving his back when she realized he had stopped and was standing completely still.

Dedication

To the man who is always my hero
and the kids who add color to my story

Chapter 1

"I've danced for the National Ballet Company for eleven years, given it everything I had. I deserve more than this!"

Elana had worked herself into a frenzy. Her voice was too loud, and her hand motions were too big. She must look ridiculous. Every absurd bounce of her tutu proved it as she paced around the cramped office, but in this moment, she couldn't restrain herself. She should have changed out of her sweaty practice uniform of a black leotard over rosy-pink tights and large flouncy tutu before coming in to this meeting—a meeting that would forever mark the end of her career as a professional dancer.

"Hey, calm down." Jason sighed and rubbed his already red eyes. He gestured to a chair in front of his desk. "Why don't you sit? You're making me nervous."

She paused for a moment, but the blood coursing through her body made it impossible to remain still. "No, thanks."

She had known about the budget problems, of course, and she had seen her dismissal looming in the distance, but now that it was happening, she found herself unable to make a dignified exit. Working at the National Ballet Company had been her life for so long that she panicked at the thought of leaving and completely redefining herself.

"We've been over this." His weary eyes followed her around the room as she paced. "There's no more money available. The Wakefield family has been our largest donor for some time now. They've covered most of our operating expenses for years, but they decided to give to other causes next year. We just don't have enough money to keep everyone in the *corps de ballet*."

He fiddled with a pile of paperweights on the corner of his desk, clutter accrued over his long years of service. He probably wanted her to accept her fate and leave, but was too professional to admit it. Well, it wasn't that simple.

She huffed and angrily wiped away the tear rolling down her cheek. She didn't want to give him the satisfaction of seeing her cry.

"And come on, honey," he continued, speaking to her like a child. He always cooed at the dancers as if they weren't grown women. It was one of her biggest pet peeves. "You're one of the oldest dancers in the corps. You'd be retiring in the next few years anyway. Yeah, you still look good, and phew, those legs! But it's time for you to move on. You can relax a bit now, maybe even have some fun. Don't you have a life you'll be happy to get back to?"

Elana bristled at his question. Of course she had a life. She had a mom who'd be happy to see more of her, some cousins scattered around the country, and a handful of friends who might be willing to reconnect, but not much else. She had dedicated herself to ballet, practicing for hours every day just to maintain top form. That dedication and persistence had cost her social life. She had turned down invitations from her friends in favor of her career so often over the years that the invitations had eventually stopped coming.

She was trying to think of a response that wouldn't expose her lack of a social life when the office door banged open and cut in on her thoughts. She froze to the spot, her body betraying her, rendered helpless by the sight of the man who had barged into the room.

He was evidently used to commanding a room. His resolute stance emphasized a suit well-tailored to accommodate his broad shoulders, and he seemed unconcerned about the possibility that he might be interrupting something important. The haphazard office, filled with odds and ends acquired through years of productions, made his crisp figure look all the more striking. When Jason saw the man, he sat up straighter.

"Mr. Wilcox, I assume?" the man asked without looking at Jason. His inscrutable eyes scanned the scene, assessing each aspect of the disorganized office, but she couldn't be sure what his conclusion was. His face was stoic. That is, until his eyes reached her. His body flinched when he turned in her direction. It was only a moment, and he soon regained his composure, but his whole manner had changed sharply for one instant.

Jason gave a quick nod. "Yes, of course. No one told me you were coming today. I'm sorry. If I'd known, I'd, well... What can I do for you, Mr. Wakefield?"

Elana would have been surprised to see Jason so flustered—that is, if she'd paid attention to him. But ever since the door swung open, she had been unable to tear her focus away from the man's piercing green eyes, framed perfectly by his flowing, cocoa hair. She had seen those eyes before, on a night last month when she had been someone other than herself. It was the end of the season party, where Jason first brought up the ballet's budget problems and hinted that some of the dancers, including her, would soon be let go. She stormed off after he told her, ready to go home and have a full-on pity party, but then a pair of emerald eyes on a mystery man in a dark corner stopped her.

They spent the entire party in that corner, getting closer as the night wore on. The attraction was immediate and insurmountable. She knew how the night would end when he first brushed his fingers down her bare shoulder, and she was willing to go with it, consequences be damned. She wanted to feel good and forget about the end of her career, and this impossibly sexy man could help her do both. She never bothered to learn anything about him beyond his first name, Bennett. The party passed in a blur of kisses, and she had taken him back to her apartment afterward. An electrifying jolt shot through her body at the memory.

Elana was so lost in her thoughts that it took a beat for her to recognize what Jason had just said. This man standing in his office, the man she thought she would never see again after that memorable night, was Bennett Wakefield, presumably of the Wakefield family that had stopped contributing to the ballet and caused her and several others to lose their jobs. As an awareness of his touch still reverberated through her body, she struggled to reignite the raging fire at her dismissal. "Excuse me!"

Both Jason and the mysterious Bennett Wakefield turned to her. She had their full attention but fumbled for words in a way she never had before, distracted by Bennett's full eyebrows slowly lifting. She had

4

performed in front of thousands, so why was one man's scrutiny this hard to overcome?

"You can't barge in here in the middle of a private meeting. We were discussing something important. You come in here like you own the place, just because you deigned to give the company some of your family's money in the past. Well that doesn't make you king."

She had to pull it together. Her indignation became more embarrassing as each word tripped out of her mouth. She needed to calm down if she wanted to be respected, but now that a one-night stand had waltzed in, that seemed impossible. Her emotions flew around unchecked, leaving chaos in their wake.

Across the room, Bennett's countenance never changed, even as her energy rose to a fevered pitch. He merely waited, eyebrows lifting ever higher, until she was done.

"I'm sorry to have interrupted," he said, his voice smooth. She was about to accept his apology, but he went on, "What's your name?"

His swift, impersonal reply knocked the wind out of her sails. He obviously wasn't as impacted by her presence as she was by his. The emotionless way he asked her name made it seem like he didn't know they had met before, much less been together in her bed. She only knew his first name, but still. She remembered him. Hell, every part of her body remembered him.

She took a step back and refocused her energy. She couldn't decide if she was angrier that Bennett had forgotten her or his family had caused her to lose her job. Logically, neither of those things were cause to be upset at him. After all, they had made no promises to each other, and his family was free to give their money to any organization they wanted.

If she had run into Bennett at any other moment, she would have been fine, but he caught her in the middle of an upsetting day, and she was unable to maintain her composure.

"I'm Elana Deveaux. I'm an old ballerina." She flinched as she said "old," realizing the second, unintended meaning. "I mean, I've been dancing with the company for years, but I just found out I've been let go." She needed to stop and take a breath. This man didn't deserve to know the personal details of her life, and she was only making herself look more pathetic as she continued rambling.

His lips fell apart, as if he had just figured something out. He clicked his tongue, and the memory of what else his tongue could do slammed into her. She couldn't let herself get distracted. Not now.

"Apparently, our donors have decided the ballet is not worth supporting anymore." She sneered, wanting him to know he had a part in her situation.

That got him. He nodded and rubbed his forehead, new creases etching their way across his brow. "I'm sorry you lost your job, but that wasn't me. You're thinking of my father." He waved at the air. "I don't have any say in the donations. I just come to the shows with my family."

Elana opened her mouth to spout some scathing insult about his father, anything to make her feel better, but she couldn't think of the words. Instead, she settled for silence and crossed arms, hoping her angry glare was leaving a mark.

"Sorry about your job, though," he added, after it became clear she wasn't going to speak.

Another lengthy silence passed, and Jason's nervous gaze shot back and forth between Elana and Bennett.

Finally, Bennett dropped his impassive stare, and his shoulders softened as he sighed. He seemed to have taken off some heavy armor weighing him down, and his body loosened. He turned to Jason. "I'm actually here about my daughter. I'm told she loves ballet."

Elana couldn't hide her confusion—why did someone have to tell him what his daughter liked?

He seemed to sense her uncertainty and spoke quickly. "I mean, she loves ballet. Doing it, watching it, you name it. Big fan."

She nodded along but wondered why he was telling her this. She wasn't ready to stop being angry, regardless of what personal stories he shared.

"I came here today to hire a private ballet teacher for my daughter. She'd also need to do occasional tutoring sessions. The tutoring won't be difficult, just making sure she does the homework her school is sending her. So, if you don't work for the ballet anymore, you can be that teacher." He spoke directly to Elana and paused for a moment, giving her a look that bordered on pleading. The kind man she had known a month ago appeared, but he vanished in an instant as Bennett transformed back into a stern, entitled businessman. "I'll make it worth your while, of course. Twice your usual pay, days off if you need them, a bonus at the end for a job well done."

She was at a loss for words. He wasn't asking. He had the gall to believe he could command her to do something and she would happily follow along like a puppy dog. He had a lot to learn. She wouldn't be bossed around by some man, no matter how rich and attractive he was.

An emphatic no was on the tip of her tongue, but she hesitated when she thought about what she had to go home to. Her mother had moved in with her last month after she lost her home to debt, and the small DC apartment was starting to feel downright crowded. That wasn't a problem when she was at the ballet more than sixty hours each week, but as much as she loved her mother, the idea of spending every waking hour together made her queasy. Plus, she had always worked and wasn't sure what to do with herself when unemployed. Why not take Bennett up on his offer and make some good money while figuring out her next career move? Maybe she could help her mom find a new place to live or pay off some debt with the unexpected income.

She was trying to be rational and consider all the reasons to either accept or turn down the job, but her mind wandered every time she felt the weight of his eyes observing her. Her head filled with different scenarios of what could happen if they saw each other more often. A dark room, lit only by those smoldering green eyes as he watched her dance. Him running his hands along her legs as he helped her stretch. A pair of crumpled pink tights on the ground next to a porcelain bathtub…

Elana's mind and body betrayed her rational side by giving in to his sex appeal. How could she be both angry and turned on at the same time? She didn't want to see him anymore, but her stomach fluttered at the idea of spending more time together. It was infuriating.

This behavior went against her normal character,

and she had to work to force the unwanted thoughts out of her mind so she could think objectively. When she finally did, the reality of her situation struck her like a punch in the gut: she had just been fired, had no job waiting for her, and was living with her mother, who was carrying a tremendous amount of debt. She couldn't afford to turn down a lucrative teaching gig, no matter how rudely it was presented and regardless of whether the man offering it was a womanizer.

"Okay, Mr. Wakefield," she grumbled in her most affronted tone. She wanted him to know she was doing this of her own free will and not because he had told her to. "I'll do it."

"That's settled, then. And please, call me Bennett."

He shook her hand, sending a shockwave up her arm and into her core. She had to fortify her knees against their sudden melting. She needed to keep reminding herself she was doing this for the money, not the man. After all, he was obviously a playboy, and a flake at that, since he didn't remember their night together.

As he left, he called, "I'll have my assistant get in touch with the details, and my housekeeper will make up a room for you in my estate. We live in a small town, and there aren't many other places to stay, so I think it would be best if you just stayed on Wakefield property."

Bennett's last words didn't sink in immediately. She was going to have to move into his house in the middle of nowhere. Her mind struggled to understand what that would mean. The hall was empty when she called after him, "Wait, what? I'm supposed to stay with you?"

****

Bennett rushed down the hallway, barely acknowledging the dancers that hopped out of his way. He needed to escape as quickly as possible after touching Elana's hand. The voltage that had permeated his body at her contact was too much, and he didn't have space in his life for romance right now. He had pretended not to know her in front of her boss to save her the embarrassment of having to explain their connection, but the sexual tension was obviously still there.

"Mr. Wakefield?" a voice behind him called, making him increase his pace. He didn't want to talk to anyone.

But the footsteps behind him picked up.

"Mr. Wakefield!"

He recognized the slightly panicked and out-of-breath voice. It was Jason. "Dammit," he huffed under his breath. Clenching his fists and turning around, he pinned a tight smile onto his face. "Sorry, Jason, I didn't hear you. What do you need?"

Jason skidded to a stop next to him and fiddled with his shirt. "Oh, nothing really, Mr. Wakefield."

He sighed as Jason continued. It always took him a few minutes to get to the point. Usually Bennett had patience for that, but not today.

"I just wanted to make sure you got everything you needed. Do you want me to do anything to help with Elana's transition to working for you?"

The mention of her name made him flinch. He didn't know what had gotten into him when he offered her the job. "No, thank you. My secretary can take care of the details," he said, turning slightly to indicate that he was ready to leave and the conversation was over.

But Jason didn't seem to notice. "I didn't know you had a daughter. How old is she?"

"Sixteen," he said, keeping his voice as flat as possible. This was not a topic he wanted to discuss. He had enough trouble trying to explain to his father how a sixteen-year-old girl had showed up on his doorstep with nothing but a suitcase and a note from a lawyer explaining she was his daughter; he definitely didn't want to talk about it with someone he barely knew.

"A teenager, huh?" Jason laughed, missing Bennett's stern tone and waiting for a response. When he received only silence, he shuffled from side to side.

"Yep," Bennett finally muttered, needing to end the conversation. A headache was beginning to hammer at his temples. "I have to go. I'm late for a meeting."

"Oh, well, okay," Jason stuttered. "Tell your father hello for me, and I'm sure your daughter will love her lessons."

Bennett turned and rushed down the tangle of halls behind the stage, the longer strands of his hair falling into his eyes with each stride. He shoved them back into place, frustrated that he was losing his composure. His father had always made it clear no matter what he felt internally, he should always present a polished front to the world. He failed at that more and more these days.

He finally reached the end of the hall, slamming the door open and escaping into the crisp fall air. He took a deep breath and released it slowly, forcing a sense of calm down to his fingertips. He had to get his family together and figure out how to be a father before he could even start to think about romance.

Unfortunately, he kept seeing a pink tutu bouncing around Elana's lithe hips. This was going to be harder than he thought.

Chapter 2

Elana had known Bennett came from a wealthy family, but nothing prepared her for the magnificence of his house. No, house was too small a word—mansion would be a more apt description. She imagined her apartment compared to the behemoth in front of her and concluded it could fit inside one bay in his garage.

The house was enormous and gaudy. Its colossal columns and opulent molding stood in marked contrast to the simple beauty of the natural surroundings. Turrets and windows seemed to appear out of nowhere all over the home, and strategically managed ivy covered some of the walls.

The mansion was the only man-made structure in sight, as if it had been plopped down in the middle of the quiet landscape. A field stretched out behind the mansion, ending with a line of trees that marked the beginning of a lush forest. Mountains flanked the property in the distance on all sides, and clouds cast gently floating shadows across the peaks. She had no idea how far the Wakefield property extended.

She drove her beat-up old car around a circular driveway bordered with double rows of manicured shrubs and stopped in front of a four-columned archway. A chandelier hung in the entrance, and a large fountain stood in the middle of the roundabout on the opposite side of where she parked. She laughed at the cherub angel in the center of the fountain. Water spilled from a pitcher the angel was holding and cascaded down in all directions. The house embodied every cliché she had imagined.

After letting the heavy brass knocker fall against the door, she straightened the wrinkles of her skirt and smoothed her disobedient curls. She wasn't used to wearing her hair down, typically opting for a tightly cinched ballerina's bun, but she had spent an embarrassingly long amount of time in the mirror last night deciding on her hair and clothes. After trying on most of her wardrobe, she had finally concluded that a flowery dress and loose, flowy hair would make her seem laid back, yet professional. The dress fell somewhere between making her look like a cool, nineties chick and making her look like a hippy. It was her go-to outfit for most daytime functions. At the time she had been confident, but now she felt inadequate. What did someone wear in a house that most likely had marble floors and solid gold accents?

The imposing door swung open, revealing an interior that reeked of old money. Everything was either deep mahogany or gold, with luxurious fabrics covering most surfaces from floor to ceiling. Even the curtains were velvet, giving the home a somber feeling. Windows covered the walls, but very little natural light came in because of the heavy fabrics. Vases and mini statues dotted every shelf and tabletop. The place looked more like a museum than a comfortable home, and she wasn't sure where people relaxed here.

Bennett strode out from behind the door to interrupt her view. He fit in perfectly with the elegant surroundings in his casual yet sophisticated button down. It looked expensive, probably custom made. She doubted he had spent any time at all debating his choice of clothing. Even his afternoon stubble was flawlessly shaped and refined. He clearly knew how to own any room.

"Come in." He reached for her suitcase. "I'm glad you found the place."

"I couldn't miss it," she replied. "Your assistant gave wonderful directions. Plus, you're the biggest house outside town. I probably could have asked anyone at the grocery store, and they'd be able to tell me the way."

He laughed. "I think you're right about that."

The mansion was situated on the outskirts of Hansbury, a small town in the middle of Virginia. Based on her quick internet search of the area, most of the townspeople seemed to work on farms and spend their free time at the local diner that became a pub at night. She had made a point to drive through the main street in town on her way here and found it charming, if a little small. The town had one grocery store, one café, one diner, and two antique stores. A few side streets held the offices for local officials and handyman. Compared to DC, Hansbury was plucked straight out of an old-timey movie, where everyone knew their neighbor and the only drama happened at the yearly fair.

She wasn't sure how he had ended up here, but she was positive this would be a huge change from the urban living she was accustomed to.

"Well, regardless. Welcome."

He flashed a smile that nearly knocked her off her feet. His pearly whites stood in marked contrast to his café au lait skin, and those damned green eyes made her feel like she was alone with him in a dimly lit room. The pleasant sensation could almost convince her to overlook that this was a man who had spent the night with her and then forgotten. Almost.

"Thanks. So where should I put my things?"

"Here, I've got it." He winked as he slid his hand over hers to pick up her suitcase.

The touch startled her, and she let go of the handle too quickly, nearly sending the bag clattering to the floor.

He caught it before it fell and smoothly set it at the bottom of a winding staircase. "Allison, the housekeeper, will take these to your room."

Elana looked around the room, relishing the opportunity to break his powerful gaze. He was so calm and self-possessed. It made her nervous, and she started talking to hide her self-consciousness. "Thanks. Well, I know you've got a lot to do, so I won't keep you from your day. I can find my way around and get myself settled."

"Don't be silly." He laughed. "I've got to give you the grand tour. You're my guest."

"Okay, then. Will I get to meet your daughter today? I'm excited to get to know her and start to set up a plan for practices. I want to learn what her goals are."

"Rose will be here soon. She's had a rough few months and tends to run on her own schedule." He appeared to think a moment and continued, "She might be, well, difficult to work with. Like I said, she's had a hard time, and she's been acting out. Getting in fights, making things up, that kind of thing. It's why I'm letting her take some time off school."

"I see." Elana nodded, wondering whether she had gotten in over her head. She had never worked with a teenager before, much less one with problems. She was about to ask him to elaborate—getting in fights and making things up sounded serious—but he didn't give her the chance. Apparently, this was a sore spot for him.

"But you don't need to start worrying about that just yet," he said, his tone getting lighter. "I'll give you a tour of the house first. There's something I've been wanting to talk to you about, anyway." He abruptly turned and walked to a hallway on his left, leaving her scurrying to keep up.

The hallway was wide and long, with antique molding adorning every border and framed art meticulously spaced at even intervals. Family portraits were sprinkled tastefully between the professional pieces, with small tables highlighting the most important pictures under small lamps. Things didn't appear to change very often around here. Everything was precise and purposeful, completely opposite the house she had grown up in.

She followed behind him, watching the seemingly unending stream of doors pass by and listening to his idle chatter about some unique feature of the house or the history of an old piece of artwork. She wasn't paying close attention until he started to talk about his family.

"This has been my family's house for generations. My dad, Rupert—that jerk who got you fired—"

He looked to her with an expectant smirk, clearly intending to make her laugh, but the wound was too raw. She could never explain to anyone how much being a ballerina had defined her, and how losing her position made her feel hopelessly unmoored.

When she didn't acknowledge his joke, he cleared his throat and continued.

"Well, the short version of the story is he inherited this house from his father who got it from his father and so on. Decades of Wakefield men. We used to farm the land, even had one of the largest herds of cattle in the region, but most people in the family have now left farming and work in business. We pretty much just maintain the estate these days and have big family reunions here every once in a while." He stopped at a doorway ahead, waiting for her to catch up. He must be used to people being intimidated by the grandness of the house. He didn't seem to mind her slowly taking in every detail.

"My older brother, Chance, is set to inherit the house when my dad dies, so I'm actually only a placeholder here until he decides he's ready to take his rightful position as the head of the family."

She thought she saw him grimace each time he mentioned his father, but she couldn't be sure. He had moved forward a few paces and was motioning inside the room.

"This is the entertainment room. Best place in the house, in my opinion. Feel free to make yourself at home. Snacks are in the back, along with some drinks if you're so inclined. And if you can think of a movie, we probably have it somewhere."

The entertainment room was as big as some of the small indie theaters she had been to during her college years. A giant screen filled one wall and several large velvet sofas were arranged so every guest would have the perfect view. Speakers were hidden around the perimeter for a full surround-sound experience, and the entire back half of the room was filled with shelves of movies, extra pillows and blankets, and a fully stocked bar. This room stood out from the rest of the house because it was designed with comfort in mind rather than grandeur. She would have to come back.

Her head spun. The maze of hallways that shaped the ground floor was disorienting, and she was sure she would get lost at least once before her contract was up. They had turned two, no, three times, and she was unsure of how to get back to the foyer. She made a mental note to take a slower walk around the house later to get her bearings.

"Where is your brother now?" she asked, attempting to make conversation while trying not to stare at the immense velvet couch in the center of the room, or to imagine what the two of them could do on it together late into the night.

"Oh, he's in New York, I think. Or maybe London. I never can keep track. He's in the business of corporate takeovers, so he goes wherever the money is. Travels almost nonstop. He's going to hate being stuck here one day." His face contorted as he talked about his brother. Apparently all of his family was a sore subject, not just Rose.

He walked past the movie screen and out onto a deck overlooking a pool with a large expanse of open field beyond it. "This is the back deck. There's a pool, a hot tub, and a sauna all at your disposal. Just ask Allison if you need help with anything."

She nodded again, feeling like a dashboard bobble head. A hot tub would soothe her sore muscles after a long, hard day of dancing. She couldn't wait to try it out. But then more thoughts about Bennett flooded in, unbidden. She twisted her hair while wondering what kind of bathing suit he wore. Long swim trunks? Tight briefs? Or maybe he was European inspired and swam without a suit.

They went back inside and continued exploring in silence, giving her ample time to pursue her daydream while appreciating his physique. His clothes hugged every line from his broad shoulders down his back, emphasizing a backside toned through years of workouts. As she watched the fabric of his shirt pull against him with each movement, she was transported to their night together, and how she had nibbled his shoulders and scratched his back. She could still taste his saltiness and hear his low, throaty sighs.

His cough brought her back to reality. She had stopped walking at some point, and he was reminding her to keep going. She smiled and continued on, cursing the hold he had over her. She needed to get past this attraction and get control of her fantasies before they impacted her work.

"So," she began, trying to think of some small talk to distract herself from him. Her erotic reveries were getting out of hand. She decided to bring up the biggest buzzkill she could think of to cool off her attraction. "Is Rose's mother here, too? When will I meet her?"

He stopped abruptly at her question, making her nearly run right into him. His jaw set into a firm line, and his hands opened and closed into fists. His manner made it clear she had asked the wrong question.

"She's not here," he said through clenched teeth, breathing hard. "You won't meet her."

Elana was equal parts relieved and curious. The way he spoke showed he wasn't together with Rose's mother, and she had to admit that was a relief.

"That's okay," she said meekly. "Just thought I'd ask."

She went to take a step forward, but he remained rooted to the spot with every muscle flexed. She watched the tension strain his body and made a mental note to not mention Rose's mother again. He took one final breath and softened.

"Of course." He turned his body to face her full on and then hesitated. "Before we go on, there's something I want to talk to you about."

Her heart pounded in her temples. What did he have to say?

"I just had to tell you…"

A loud crash behind a swinging door up ahead interrupted his sentence.

"I better go check that out," he grumbled, raising his hands and eyebrows in a frustrated shrug. "Wait here. I'll be back. That's the door to the kitchen, so it's probably just Allison, but she might need help."

She had nowhere to go, so she studied the pictures in the hallway, trying to slow her racing heartbeat. She focused on each picture, examining all the boring details to calm herself down.

Images of perfect families over various time periods filled the walls. The families always posed in front of the same towering oak tree. The Wakefields must take pride in their home and their lineage. She identified Bennett in one picture. He was with two other men near his age, and they were each sitting on a horse wearing matching white polos and leather riding boots.

The men all had the same dark hair and piercing eyes, an obvious family resemblance. This photo stood out from the others, though, because the men were actually smiling.

"Those are my brothers."

She jumped as he snuck up behind her. His voice was so close the vibrations on her neck gave her chills.

"Chance is on my left, and Peter is next to him. Chance is the one I was talking about earlier. The tycoon."

"You guys must have been the three musketeers growing up," she said, scooting away to avoid his nearness. "You look like you got into all sorts of trouble."

"I guess so." He seemed to be thinking. "We're all very different people now."

"Well, Chance is the businessman, so who are you and Peter?"

"Peter is the free spirit, I suppose. He lives in San Diego. Yoga by day, tortured writing by night."

She laughed at the image. It was almost impossible to imagine any of the aristocratic men in front of her doing yoga. But he had turned back to the picture, grim.

"My dad let him off the hook from needing to have some noteworthy career because he's the baby of the family. I'm a different story." He sighed. "I'm the nerdy computer guy. Apps, actually. Like what you have on your phone. It's why I can live here and watch over the house for everyone. I can code from anywhere, so Dad figured I could babysit the family estate while Chance was out building his fortune and Peter was writing the next great American novel. I don't think he really understands what I do. Just that I don't have an imposing office or an impressive title."

She was suddenly sorry for him. He looked sad in the shadow of all those formidable family photos. Sad but determined.

"Anyway, we can talk more about my complicated family later." He turned back to her. "We have plenty of time to get to know each other."

A thrill shot through her body as she thought about the long weeks to come in close proximity to him. She had agreed to a three-month term—enough to get through the holidays. Then they'd revisit her contract after seeing how the arrangement was working out. But she wasn't sure how she was going to focus while living and working in such close quarters.

As if reading her mind, he said, "I do want to talk to you about one personal matter, though."

She waited in anticipation.

"You were mad at me in the office the other day."

"No, I wasn't." She tried to look shocked and confused, but knew she was failing. She was embarrassed by her behavior and didn't want Bennett to get at the reason she'd been angry, that she'd lashed out after being hurt by his indifference to her. "I was just in a bad mood because I was out of a job all of a sudden."

"Yeah, it was bad timing on my part to interrupt, but I think you were also mad at me. I just wanted to say…"

Another door slammed, this time behind them.

"Dammit," he huffed under his breath, slapping a palm against his thigh. "What is it now?"

****

Bennett turned to stare directly into his daughter's clear green eyes. She winced at his exclamation, and he cursed internally. The last thing he needed right now was to injure her even more.

"I'm sorry, Rose." He was flustered. "I didn't realize it was you."

"Yeah, sure," she mumbled, looking down and kicking a large antique table.

"Hey, I want you to meet Elana, your new ballet teacher. She just got in today, and I'm giving her the grand tour."

He gestured toward Elana, and she stepped forward to shake Rose's hand, but the teenager didn't look up. Instead, she swatted at the items on the tabletop.

"Nice to meet you, Rose," Elana said, a thin smile plastered on her lips. She was clearly trying to sound cheerful but not succeeding. He wouldn't be able to help her connect with Rose, though, because he still hadn't gotten past her defenses himself.

"Yeah, sure," Rose repeated, her voice somehow flatter than before. "Can I take a car? I don't know anyone, and there's nowhere to go in this stupid town, but I need to get out of the house. I'm going crazy stuck in here all the time."

"Of course," he replied, wanting to smooth things over. Giving Rose a car was a tangible thing he could do for her, at least. "The keys are all hanging on a rack on the wall in the garage. Take any car you want."

He watched her leave. She swung her arms too wide and hit every obstacle she could reach in the hallway, knocking one freestanding picture frame so hard that it slid and came to rest perilously close to the edge of an end table. He wasn't sure how to win her over—teenagers were an entirely different species—but he had to keep trying until he did. He sighed and once again turned to Elana.

"I'm sorry about that. Teenagers, what can you do?" He shrugged and tried to chuckle, but the sound caught in his throat.

"Yeah, teenagers," she mumbled.

They stood there in silence with him not knowing what else to say. He had been attempting to apologize for pretending not to know her and acting so cold in the office, to explain he was only trying to save her some embarrassment, but the moment had passed. Rose left a heavy shadow on his mood, and she was his primary concern. Maybe it was better if Elana stayed angry at him and thought he was a bad guy. Then he wouldn't have to worry about the intense pull he felt toward her.

When Elana had come into his home, he had been drawn to her as if she were magnetic. She was a burst of fresh air in this stale mansion, bringing life into his old family home and oozing sensuality.

His fingers twitched as they longed to reach out and slide between the strands of her hair, and he was trying not to imagine what he would do to her behind any of these closed doors if given the chance. He was being as professional as he could be.

After a moment's hesitation, he opted not to address the misunderstanding from the office for now. He'd let Elana think he was a jerk playboy who'd forgotten her and use that as a defensive shield against their attraction. That way, he could concentrate on his relationship with Rose.

"I'll just take you to your room." He exhaled, needing to breathe air not filled with her scent. "You've had a long day, and we can finish the tour later."

Chapter 3

Elana was surprised; Rose was actually a decent ballerina. After their first uncomfortable meeting in the hallway, she had expected a bored, rich girl who didn't want to practice and had zero interest in listening to the instructions of a new teacher. But Bennett had been right when he said Rose loved ballet. She was willing to do all the combinations Elana suggested. And she transformed into a completely different person when Bennett wasn't in the room. Sometimes she even smiled.

Elana had never seen a home with a ballet studio custom built in one of the rooms. Bennett obviously retrofitted an extra space just for Rose. The studio had a sweeping wall covered in mirrors, a barre stretching along two sides, and professional-grade ballet flooring. Matching the impeccable quality and attention to detail in the rest of the house, it was nicer than some of the studios she had grown up dancing in. He even had a selection of classical music she could play on a built-in sound system. He had put a lot of time and effort, not to mention money, into providing anything they might need.

She imagined the kind of practice space she would build if she had unlimited resources for the job. This aligned closely with the ballet studio of her dreams.

"Nice toe point," she called to Rose from the

opposite side of the room. Rose was working on a simple across-the-floor combination they had created together. She wanted to see what kind of moves inspired her and was building their first class off those. Plus, she was trying to keep her directions simple and her corrections positive until they knew each other better. In a few weeks, though, she'd turn into a tougher teacher and really whip Rose into shape.

"Try to move with your spine as straight as possible. Imagine a string connected to the top of your head pulling your body up toward the ceiling."

Rose nodded and headed back to her starting position to repeat the combination.

They had been at it for the better part of two hours, and Elana's muscles ached. When the song ended, she leaned against the barre.

"Let's call it a day," she said brightly, not wanting her student to know how unusually tired she was. She couldn't show weakness in her first week. "Come over to the barre, and we'll stretch out before leaving."

"Sure." Rose shrugged and shuffled over. The sullen teenager act returned as soon as she stopped dancing. She grabbed the railing and bent forward to stretch her shoulders.

"What did you think of the class?" She was determined to make a good impression, but she was nervous.

"It was fine. You're like my old teacher in a lot of ways. Except she came down on me harder when we had private lessons." Rose didn't look up as she talked. She shifted her weight and put one leg up on the barre.

"Oh, I didn't know you had another private teacher." The way Bennett had described the job made it seem like he had never hired a ballerina before. She'd have to ask him about it later so he could fill her in on what they had worked on. "Your dad didn't tell me that."

Rose stiffened at the word "dad" and snorted. "Bennett," she nearly growled, "wouldn't know anything about my old teacher. He's only been my father for a few months."

She wasn't sure what to say, or even what that meant. She remembered his odd word choice—*I'm told she loves ballet*—and something clicked into place in her mind. Unsure of whether to pursue this line of questioning, she merely mumbled an acknowledgement and continued stretching. She didn't want to force Rose into talking about a painful subject, not when they were just getting to know each other.

Rose straightened and shifted onto her other leg, placing her foot higher up on the barre. "He wasn't around when I was growing up, you know. My mom said he never wanted a kid. He left when I was little." She quickly flicked her eyes up to meet Elana's and then turned away. "Now my mom is dead, and I'm stuck here with that jerk."

Rose's blunt honesty startled Elana. She had never been in this situation before, with a teenager spilling her heart out. She was about to reach out and hug her, or at least express her sympathy, when Rose slammed her foot down and started walking away.

"Anyway, whatever," she huffed. "I'm here now. That's that. It sucks, but there's nothing I can do about it." She grabbed her bag, flung it over her shoulder, and left without another word.

The door slammed shut before Elana could process

the interaction. It had happened so fast she hadn't been able to respond to Rose's story. She was still sitting on the floor, legs askew and bent in half. The poor girl had been through so much and was clearly having a hard time. She would have to do her best to make things easier for her.

She tried to think back to when her father had left their family. She had been angry, just like Rose, but what had she needed? The answer was clear: she had needed her mother. When things got tough, she had always turned to her mom, a pattern she still followed to this day. But Rose said her mother had died, so now she was all alone. She couldn't imagine how hard that must be. The pouting and behavioral problems Bennett had mentioned made perfect sense.

She continued to think about Rose while she finished stretching, but then her thoughts drifted to Bennett, and she got angry. Who did he think he was? Since her father left when she was young, she didn't have any sympathy for deadbeat dads. It was bad enough he had forgotten her after their one-night stand, but this was too much. He could be the most handsome man in the world, and damn if he didn't have a perfect smile, but she couldn't be with a man who didn't take care of his family.

As her frustration built, her muscles twitched with the extra energy. She always had a physical reaction to her emotions, and the only way to let it out was by dancing. She had always been able to forget problems or distract herself from events in her life by getting lost in music. Along with her mother, dance was her only other constant.

She looked around to make sure Rose had left,

Riley Blair

connected her phone to the speaker, and turned on the latest single as loud as it would go. It was an acoustic song about a woman who had been wronged by a man. Perfect for her mood.

Standing up, she began swaying, slowly first and then building her movements with the melody. Her hips led her body, and her ballet shoes gently tapped against the floor as she slithered from one spot to the next, ending against the wall. Closing her eyes, she raised her hands above her, letting one leisurely slide the length of her arm, then around her neck, and down across her breasts and stomach. She bent over to allow her hand to finish its route, tracing one leg. The song ended, and another, faster one took its place.

The melody began, and a techno beat echoed off the walls. She smiled. This was exactly what she needed—a sickly-sweet pop song to get stuck in her head and drown out her other thoughts.

As the song picked up, she progressed from calm nodding to full on flailing around—the kind of dancing she did in the privacy of her own home when nobody was watching. She wanted to drop her proper ballerina persona for a few minutes and transform into someone else. Someone without a care in the world. She was kicking, shaking her head, and snapping in every direction, until she noticed the dark figure in the doorway.

****

Bennett couldn't bring himself to interrupt. He had intended to ask Elana how her first day went after he saw Rose fleeing the studio, but then a svelte figure slinking around the room greeted him as he came through the door. He should have backed away right

30

then and there and given her privacy, but he had never seen a woman move like that before. Sure, he went to dance clubs and had even seen a stripper or two in his time, but this was different. These were the movements of a classically trained dancer dropping the pretense and simply letting her body flow with the music.

Her body moved in one smooth motion, a slow wave beginning at her toes and travelling through her curved hips, taut stomach, and perky breasts. He watched as she leaned against the wall and let her hand roam her figure. His own fingers stirred and drew paths along his thighs as he imagined his hands discovering each part of her. His mind flashed back to their night together and how he had gently traced her form.

He flushed involuntarily, remembering the way he had clumsily slid her strappy black dress to the floor. He had fumbled at first, intimidated by her poise and tight figure. But after the initial stumble, they'd immediately fallen into sync. He had never craved a woman so much, and it felt like she needed him, too.

The music changed sharply, and the loud bass of a pop song knocked him out of his reverie. He almost hooted as she kicked her legs and shook out every limb, but he didn't want to give himself away. He was about to quietly escape when she froze and stared at him.

"Geez," she said breathlessly. "Heart attacks run in my family, you know. You could have killed me!" And then she demanded, "How long have you been standing there?"

"I'm sorry," he started, walking into the studio with his hands out. The click of his dress shoes resonated on the studio floor, adding to the cacophony still spilling out of the speakers. She put one finger up and jogged to her phone, abruptly shutting off the music. The resulting silence made him feel oddly exposed.

"I didn't mean to scare you. I was just coming to ask about your day. I haven't been here long. Promise." His words came out stilted, awkward. "I like your moves, but I hope you're not teaching them to my daughter."

He gave an exaggerated wink, but her face colored and then darkened. All of his attempts at joking since she got here had crashed and burned. When had he become such a putz?

She frowned and started to gather her things. He was clearly out of her good graces. "I'm not. Don't worry."

He mentally kicked himself and vowed to start fresh. Things weren't going well for him, and he didn't need to dig himself deeper in the hole.

"Hey, sorry." He put his hand on the small of her back as she bent over packing. She flinched slightly in response but didn't acknowledge his hand. "I didn't mean to make fun. You really are a good dancer, and I'm sure you're an even better teacher for Rose."

"Well, thank you for the vote of confidence." She stood with her bag, ready to leave. "Is that all?"

"I guess so." He shrugged as she started to walk away. "Hey?" he said quickly, needing to do something to repair what was broken so they could at least be friends. He owed it to Rose to make things go as smoothly with her teacher as possible. If they continued on like this, the next three months were going to be terrible for everyone. At least, that was the reason he was telling himself.

She turned, looking at him with eyebrows raised. When she didn't say anything, he swallowed hard and said what he knew he should, even though she was making it incredibly difficult with her icy glare.

"I just wanted to say I had a good time at that party. You know, the ballet's end of the season party? A few months ago?"

At his confession, her arms unfolded and her mouth slipped slightly ajar, making her full lips look more inviting, if that was possible.

Scratching the back of his neck and looking down to distract himself from her lips, he continued, "Well, anyway, I just thought you should know that."

She stood motionless, her expression unreadable.

He didn't know what he hoped to get from her, since he couldn't handle any kind of romantic involvement right now, but he at least wanted her to stop being so angry. If nothing else, they needed to have a friendly professional relationship. For Rose, of course. Plus, he had to admit a part of him wanted to see her eyes light up as they had the night of the party. She made his testosterone shoot through the roof with just one look of appreciation, and he craved that high again.

Since the silence was dragging on without any indication she would respond, he strode to the door and held it open for her.

"I'll let you go now."

She stepped forward but then hesitated. When she finally spoke, her words were slow, careful. "You...remember me from that night? I thought you had forgotten me."

How could she think he had forgotten her? No man

in his right mind could forget the way she used every inch of her body to drive him to the point of ecstasy. She had pulled him in with an invisible force the first night they were together, and he was coming to realize the effect hadn't worn off. She still held sway over him.

"Of course! There's no way I could forget that night."

"But you asked who I was when you hired me," she stammered, furrowing her brows. "You acted like we had never met before. You asked me my name!"

He sniffed and pushed his sleeves up, feigning confidence to hide the nervousness she made him feel. "I didn't want to embarrass you in front of your boss, so I pretended we had never met. I didn't want to force you into an awkward admission at work. But then you blamed me for getting you fired. I thought letting your boss in on our little secret would stoke your hostile fire even more."

She was still staring at him with a look of disbelief. Her head was cocked to one side, with a few strands of hair slipping out from her bun and sliding down her face. He wanted to reach out and grab her chin, pulling her close and kissing her again to show her just how much he hadn't forgotten.

"Well, that was…thoughtful, I guess." She appeared to believe him, but seemed reluctant to admit it. He wasn't sure why—what else had he done?

"Plus, I have a reputation to protect as a serious man, too, you know. I'm not typically in the habit of having one-night stands with beautiful dancers and then leaving them alone in their beds early in the morning. I've actually never been involved with someone from the ballet." He paused to let his words sink in. She needed to know she hadn't been part of a parade of women or another trophy on his shelf. He smiled as her cheeks colored. "I just wanted you to know. In case that was why you have it out for me."

She laughed, finally breaking her stoic facade. "I don't have it out for you. I mean, that's nice to know, but it doesn't change anything. I'm your daughter's ballet teacher. I'm here for her."

"What a coincidence, so am I!" He overemphasized his words in mock amazement. He swelled with pride at the small smile his words coaxed onto her lips. "So...we're friends, then?" He slid toward her, hand out like they were closing a business deal.

"Friends," she agreed cautiously.

They clasped hands to shake on it, but the silly gesture suddenly turned serious. Her doe eyes hooked him and reeled him in. An electric current ran unbroken through her fingers and up his arm, causing his stomach to quake and his manhood to take notice.

As if controlled by an outside force, his free hand swept behind her, urging her toward him. His hand rested on the arch of her back as she offered only the slightest resistance. A small voice in his head whispered he shouldn't get any more involved with his daughter's ballet teacher than he already was, but that voice was instantly drowned out as she let out an indistinct moan. He couldn't fight her pull. He was falling down the rabbit hole, and he had to kiss her.

Letting go of her hand, he grabbed her chin as he had imagined earlier and drew her lips to his.

****

Bennett was kissing her, a deep, forceful kiss that

made Elana forget for a moment who she was. She could only focus on the warmth of his body and the pressure of his lips against her own. His growing erection surged against her stomach, and she was keenly aware of her lack of clothing, both regretting and being grateful that the thin leotard she was wearing allowed her to feel his entire shape. Her own nipples hardened in response.

The urgency of their kiss pulled her focus back to her lips, but her senses were slowly returning, and with them, a growing awareness that she shouldn't be doing this.

She pushed him away and gasped for breath, licking the slightly salty flavor of his skin off her lips. His eyes were hungry and resolute. He intended to embrace her again. She turned away to break the trance.

"We shouldn't be doing this," she mumbled.

"I know. I just can't help myself when I'm around you."

He was slowly positioning himself behind her. The heat of his breath sent tremors down her spine, and her stomach involuntarily shivered in anticipation of his hand coming to rest there.

"I can't be distracted by romance, either," he whispered into her ear. "I need to focus on Rose right now. I really want her to feel at home here after what happened with her mother. Did she tell you?"

Elana twitched and closed her lips. "Yes," she said, instantly remembering what Rose had said. This man was a jerk who didn't raise his own daughter, and she needed to steer clear of him. She picked his hand up from where it had travelled on her thigh and stepped away.

He looked surprised at her brusque response. "I didn't mean we needed to talk about the whole messy situation now. We can discuss it later if you'd like."

"No, no. It's time for me to go anyway," she insisted, backing away.

He looked dumbfounded and more than a little disappointed, but that wasn't her concern. She had to protect herself from getting more involved with this jerk. The first night had been a mistake, and this kiss was another slip, but she had enough willpower to resist him. Didn't she?

Grabbing her bag once again, she strode to the door. "I'll see you later." She bolted and ran down the never-ending hall, with his stunned face floating in her mind.

Once safely hidden in her room, she collapsed against the bedframe. She needed some space to think. Bennett had an intangible quality that clouded her thoughts and made her forget reason. Plus, she wasn't feeling very well and had other suspicions she needed to figure out.

She was glad he hadn't forgotten about their incredible night together. It was actually kind of chivalrous for him to try to preserve her dignity in front of her boss. She shouldn't have been so aggressive toward him and jumped to conclusions. But she couldn't forget Rose's story of abandonment. If he was the kind of man who could leave his child without a second thought, then he wasn't a man she wanted to be with.

With a sigh, she dug deep in her suitcase, searching for the thing she had been avoiding since she arrived. She grasped the pregnancy test and slowly pulled it out.

It was time to figure out just how much his character would matter to her. She took the test into the bathroom and waited for her answer.

For two minutes, Elana paced around the bedroom, running her hand slowly across each plush fabric or intricately carved edge. She flopped down at the huge writing desk next to the window, but then, unable to sit still, immediately got up again. The large bedroom suddenly felt suffocating, and it was all she could do not to start crying.

The possibility of pregnancy had crossed her mind the day before leaving Washington DC. It was not something she had been expecting, and before that day, she had rarely allowed herself to think about children in her future. Kids usually spelled the end of a career for professional ballerinas, and so the dancers never talked about their hopes for families. But she reminded herself she was no longer a professional ballerina.

After what felt like an eternity, she looked at the result—positive. A mix of emotions flooded her system. The doubt from a moment before was replaced with a brief panic. She wanted children eventually, but this was totally unanticipated. She had always imagined doing things in the typical order—dating, marriage, then kids—and so she wasn't sure what her new future would look like. Bennett hadn't wanted his first child; would he want this one? And would she even want to do this with him?

She began pacing around the room. Her breath came in ragged gulps, and her head swam as she tried to process her feelings. She could handle a child by herself if she had to, but the idea made her more than a little anxious. She needed to know more about what kind of man Bennett was and determine whether he had room in his life for her and their child.

Finally sensing the beginning of a plan, she relaxed a little and felt a hint of acceptance. She sat down on the edge of the bed and put her head in her hands. She wouldn't tell Bennett about the baby yet. Instead, she'd use her time in his house to learn more about him and decide what kind of parenting situation they could manage together.

A sense of purpose surged through her, and she laid back on the sheets. She knew what she had to do to move forward; she just hoped she had enough time to work everything out.

Chapter 4

"Act normal, act normal, act normal…"

That had been Elana's mantra ever since finding out she was pregnant. It worked for the most part, but every now and then she would forget about the baby for a moment, and then the realization would sneak up and knock her off her feet.

A week had passed since their encounter in the studio, and she had resumed her professional demeanor with Bennett. They saw each other almost daily, passing in the halls or exchanging pleasantries over breakfast in the morning, but their lives were largely separate. She couldn't decide whether that made her happy or disappointed. The attraction between them was undeniable, but she deliberately built up an emotional barricade to combat it. She needed to figure out a way to get to know him as a future co-parent without forgetting his shady past. And she definitely couldn't fall for him.

She grabbed a container of lavender lotion off the dresser and absentmindedly rubbed her shoulder in large, slow circles. The motion felt good, but she longed for something more soothing. The stress of the last few days had taken a toll on her body.

For days, she had been dreaming of cool ripples floating across the pool gently massaging her. But so far, she had avoided going to the pool because she didn't want to seem too forward or run into Bennett when her defenses were down. The clear blue water taunted her every time she walked past the back deck, calling out for her to jump in for a quick dip. The water could help heal her body and pacify her soul. She needed to get over her hang ups and just go for a swim.

Moving quickly so she wouldn't have time to talk herself out of it, she threw on a small black bikini, grabbed a towel, and headed toward the pool. It was time for her to start enjoying the amenities that living in a mansion afforded. After all, how often would she have the opportunity to relax in a private pool any time she wanted once she went back to her old life?

As soon as she stepped onto the deck, her muscles relaxed. She stood motionless, enjoying the breeze tracing gentle strokes across her bare skin. She closed her eyes and let the sounds of nature surround her, trying to remember when she had last escaped the hustle of the city. She hadn't gone on a real vacation in years and could barely remember the last time she truly unwound. Most of her days were spent inside the four walls of a studio, and the country landscape was a tranquil change.

A full moon illuminated the pool so it reflected softly wavering light onto everything, giving the deck an otherworldly feel. The trees were hardly visible in the distance, and the only movement on the horizon came from a lone flock of birds drifting away. The eerie light and vague boundaries combined to form the distinct impression that the house was floating in an abstract painting.

The house was so isolated that her perception of time changed. It would be easy to forget life in the city continued on in her absence, and in just six months everything would transform forever. Her hand slid to her stomach, which was still flat and hiding her secret. She let her guard down, and for only a moment, allowed herself to imagine the warmth of holding a baby in her arms. Her baby. Despite the drama, that would be a happy event. She smiled.

She was still in a state of openness when she sensed movement a few yards away on the other end of the pool. Something was gliding through the water toward her.

As Elana recognized the dark form, she mentally withdrew, her smile slipping away. She turned to creep back in the house unnoticed but stopped. She needed to get to know Bennett. It wasn't a choice right now. She had to let him in a little bit, but she'd make sure to always remember his past. Then she could decide. With effort, she forced herself to lower her defenses just a little.

"Hey, there," Bennett said when he finally arrived at the edge of the pool. "I was beginning to think you'd never leave your room. But here you are, proving me wrong." He flashed a lethal grin and winked.

In the short time they had known each other, he had winked at her three times, which was three more times than anyone else. She had always thought winking was the cheesiest thing a man could do, but when he did it, she wasn't so put off.

A smile flitted across her face. "Here I am." She laughed awkwardly, raising her hands in a half-hearted surrender. She was fighting the urge to leave but wanted to appear comfortable. "Did I interrupt your swim? Sorry. I can go and come back later if—"

"Oh no, no, of course not," he interjected. "I told you, my house is your house. Feel free to use everything it has to offer. It's one of the perks of the job."

"Okay." They stared at each other over a long silence. She didn't know what else to say, so she fiddled with the strings of her suit instead of speaking. Her feet were rooted to the ground by the side of the pool, rendering her unable to move forward.

"Well, I could use the company." He finally broke the trance, releasing them both to move again. He floated back toward the middle of the pool.

She watched the water lap against his chest and flushed, despite the soft wind. The tiny hairs on her arm stood on end, and she rubbed them earnestly in response.

He chattered as he glided away. "This is a big house in the middle of nowhere. It can get lonely when you're here by yourself."

She folded her towel carefully on a chair, delaying getting into the pool with him while savoring the anticipation. Her body buzzed at the thought of their nearly naked bodies sharing the same water. She took a deep breath and walked to the steps. The weight of Bennett's gaze followed her as she strode around the edge, illuminating her as if she were under a spotlight.

"Rose has been doing well in practice," she said, distracting herself from his gaze while purposefully sticking to the one safe topic.

"Oh? I'm glad to hear it." He smiled at the sky as he floated on his back, the stars mirrored in his eyes. "Are you getting along well?"

"Yeah, she's a great kid, really."

And it was true. Rose was always willing to put in extra effort, and she truly enjoyed ballet, something they had in common. Elana turned to him, surprised he had stopped floating. He was intensely focused on her, as if he wanted her to keep going. He seemed to crave information about his daughter.

"She's getting better every day. Her pirouettes have noticeably improved in the last week. She has a natural aptitude for dance. Has she talked to you about it at all?"

"A little, but not much. It's hard for me to get through to her. She likes you for sure, though." They had come together in the middle of the pool and were bobbing together in a wide circle. "How's my pirouette?"

Without warning, he launched himself out of the water and spun around. His muscular arms formed a strained oval above his head before slamming back down into the pool and sending a wave crashing into her face.

"Ah!" She jumped back and wiped her dripping eyes. She laughed, despite herself. "It could use some work. Your form isn't tight enough. Not quite ready for the big leagues yet, I'm afraid."

Bennett's eyes opened wide before they filled with humor. He took a stroke forward and wiped the stream of water droplets running down her cheek. Her breath caught at the unexpected touch.

He put his head down in feigned apology and grinned up at her through raised eyebrows. "Perhaps you could help me improve my technique? Maybe I could get a private lesson?"

The flirty banter snapped her back into reality. She

had to shut it down and remember he was a man she shouldn't get any more romantically entwined with. The boundaries of their relationship were clearly defined in her head, but her body always had other plans.

"I'm sure Rose could help you with your technique," she said.

"Hmm." Bringing the conversation back to his relationship with Rose made him turn serious, too.

Well, good. That was what she had been trying to achieve, wasn't it? But if so, why did the blood drain out of her face as he lowered his hand from her cheek?

"She's kind of a closed book, you know? Doesn't talk to me much."

She was about to make a biting remark about his absence during her childhood, but the pained look in his eyes made her hold her tongue. Instead, she just waited for him to continue.

He skimmed his hand over the top of the water while furrowing his brow. The light shimmered between his green eyes and the water, which was the only thing moving in the heavy silence. She would let him have his moment.

"Rose and I have a complicated relationship." He sighed. "As you know, I wasn't always there for her."

She automatically stiffened at his mention of the past, remembering Rose's story of abandonment, but she consciously pushed that out of her mind and forced herself to be open to his words. She needed to hear his side of the story, so she nodded and remained floating smoothly along.

"I'm trying to build a better relationship with her. I really am. I know she loves ballet, and so I thought..."

He faltered while he let his hands sink in the water to his sides. "I thought hiring you might be a way to get through to her and brighten her days. I want the experience of living with me to be a good one."

She didn't know how to respond. His wide eyes were searching hers, pleading for reassurance, but she wasn't sure how she could give that. She couldn't be his emissary to Rose, not if what Rose said about him was true. There was no way for her to be a good teacher to Rose if he had other, more personal expectations of her.

"I'm not sure what to say, I—"

He interrupted her. "I don't mean to put any pressure on you. That's not why I'm telling you this. I don't expect you to be involved in our relationship at all. The ballet lessons are my gift for her. To make her happy." He paused. "I just wanted you to understand that I'm trying. I'm trying to be a good father, but she won't let me do it directly, so I'm trying to make this house a place she can feel safe."

Elana needed a moment to compose herself. He was exposing his most vulnerable thoughts to her, but why? She was his employee, and he had no obligation to explain his reasons for hiring her. Once she got past the shock of his honesty, she thought about what he had said. He was trying to repair things with his daughter. But could that be enough to counteract his past actions?

The pool was suddenly small and hot. She floated away from him, gliding toward the edge.

"I'm sure you're doing your best," she stammered. "Like I said, she's a great kid." She would need to consider his words and what they could mean for her later, when he wasn't so close and his emerald eyes weren't drilling into her. His proximity and emotional openness were making her forget all the reasons she should be keeping her distance.

Bennett trailed in the water behind her, and his presence sent shivers down her spine that ended below her bikini.

"She definitely is. We agree on that much." He touched her shoulder, causing her to spin around, startled. "I didn't mean to get so serious. It's just that Rose is all I can think of lately. Like I told you before, she's my primary concern right now."

****

Bennett sighed and ducked under the water. He needed to clear his head. He didn't want to unload all of his personal drama on her, but something about her made him want to explain himself. She held sway over him, and he wasn't sure why. It was more than just the intense physical attraction and their previous night together. After all, he had experienced passion with other women before, but he hadn't told them his deepest feelings and emotions. He stayed underwater, relishing the penetrating silence only water could provide, until he couldn't hold his breath any longer.

When he came back up, the tension from the previous conversation had dissipated. Elana was kicking around on her back at the other end of the pool, staring into the sky with unfocused eyes. He marveled that she could glide through the water as smoothly as she danced on the stage. That grace never left her movements. She carried herself like she was performing at all times, and that demanded an audience.

"Let's move on to lighter topics," he called across the waves. "Tell me about your family. You learned so much about mine, but I don't know anything about yours."

"Well, my family is pretty simple." She remained on her back, flicking water gently toward the sky as she spoke. "It's just my mom and I in DC. She lives with me for now. We're pretty close, actually. She's one of my best friends and the person I turn to when I have a problem."

"That's great." He was still truly happy for her, even though he suffered a pang of envy thinking about his stunted relationship with his father. "I'm always somewhat jealous of people who can be that close with their parents. I don't think it's in the cards for my father and I, but it's what I want eventually with Rose."

Rose's image flashed in his mind, and for the first time since she had come to stay with him, he entertained an optimistic view of their future. He could envision a day, if he tried hard enough, when Rose would look at him with love and happiness. He filed the thought away for later and focused back on Elana's words.

"My cousins and I are very close, too, although none of them live within 250 miles of me. We're scattered all over the country," she continued. "There are six of us—five girls and only one guy."

"That poor man. He's completely outnumbered." He chuckled. "Growing up with only brothers, I can't imagine being surrounded by that many women."

"I don't think he minded very much," she answered. "If nothing else, potential girlfriends had to pass all sorts of tests to get through us, so he didn't get played very often."

"Makes sense, I guess."

"We all get along great and still see each other in a big group a few times a year, even though we live all over the country. We were especially tight as kids. Caused trouble at every holiday event. In fact, our parents called us the Jumping Jacks because we got so hyper when we were together. That name kind of stuck. We still use it to this day."

"The Jumping Jacks. Sounds like a peppy exercise society," he mused, laughing at himself. "Did you have a slogan, too?"

She flipped over so quickly that he jumped back in surprise.

"No!" she exclaimed, with an embarrassed look on her face.

He wasn't sure what he'd said, but this was a face of hers he'd never seen, so he would go with it. "You sure?" he nudged.

"Well, not a slogan, exactly." She shrugged, and then added, "Do you want to see something ridiculous?" in a conspiratorial voice.

"Of course." He raised one eyebrow as he drifted toward her. This night was turning out to be way more intriguing than he had anticipated when he came out for a solo swim. "What kind of ridiculous are we talking about?"

"Ah, never mind." She giggled. "I can't show you. It's too embarrassing." She closed her eyes and fell back underneath the water.

Bennett watched her body slip toward the far end of the pool. Who was this girl? She was loose and joking around, talking to him like a buddy and not an adversary. He made a mental note to talk about her family more often. It was clearly a happy topic for her.

Her features were relaxed, and her movements had become large and sweeping. Her excitement was contagious and disarmed him.

He dove under the water after her, swimming until his fingertips brushed the sides of her arms. Both froze for a moment, weightlessly suspended, before he grabbed her and pulled her back above the water.

"You're not getting off that easy," he cautioned, maintaining a light grip on her hips. "You don't offer a man something ridiculous and then just back out with no explanation. It's not fair."

Water dripped from her hair, tracing paths around each cheek, then met under her chin and flowed down through the middle of her collarbone. He reached out to wipe a loose strand of hair back, wanting to make her more comfortable but not wanting to break the uninterrupted trail of water that traversed her skin. His hand dropped, and he had to look away.

"Okay, fine. But you have to promise not to laugh too hard. I'm trusting you with an important family secret." She looked him straight in the eye with a don't-mess-with-me stare.

He nodded in compliance and held up three fingers. "Scout's honor."

"You also have to release your grip on me if you want me to be able to move," she scolded and looked down pointedly.

His eyes followed her gaze. One of his hands was still wrapped around her hip. He hadn't realized he was still holding her. She laughed as he let go dramatically and floated backward.

"Like I said, the Jumping Jacks didn't have a slogan." She halted, blushing.

He was not going to interrupt her now, not if it meant derailing whatever she was about to tell him.

She closed her eyes and admitted, "But we did have a cheer." Her voice was barely more than a whisper, as though other people were around to hear and this was a secret for his ears only. She was speaking so softly the wind carried her words away, and he could only just make out their meaning.

"You had a...cheer? Like cheerleaders?" he asked. That was not at all what he thought her ridiculous secret would be. She didn't look like any of the superficial cheerleaders he had known in high school. And she didn't strike him as particularly bubbly, either.

"No! Not like cheerleaders. I'm a ballerina, remember? We don't have very much respect for cheerleaders. More like a group of kids who had a lot of time to kill during the endless family get-togethers." She gave a mock-offended look at his suggestion, but she finally shrugged, relenting. "But fine, okay. Yes, like cheerleaders. The Jumping Jacks had a kind of anthem. We made it up after Thanksgiving dinner when I was eight or nine while the adults were all in the kitchen cleaning up and washing dishes. It just kind of stuck. One of those comforting things from childhood that you cling to well after you've entered adulthood."

"So?" He leaned forward as if he were her accomplice in some illegal activity. "Let's see it."

****

Elana couldn't believe she was going to show him the sacred Jumping Jacks cheer. She had performed in front of hundreds of people so many times before she had lost count, but this was different. Not only was it embarrassing, it was personal. But despite that, she

51

enjoyed a small thrill at sharing one of her most meaningful and cherished family memories with Bennett.

She was usually calm and reserved, but always opened up and became silly when talking about her family. They were her happy place. Plus, acting proper and professional all the time was getting tiring. She needed to do something spontaneous, even if it made her look ridiculous.

She took a deep breath and lowered her face, backing up until she felt the pool wall behind her. She was about to start when she raised her eyes and held up her hand.

"Two things," she called out, suddenly a schoolteacher disciplining her class.

Bennett raised his eyebrows.

"One, no making fun of me. You were a kid once, and I'm sure there are lots of embarrassing stories about what you did with your friends. We were all under ten when we made this, so the lyrics aren't very...how can I put it? Refined."

"Yes, ma'am. I'll lower my expectations." He smirked and gave an over-exaggerated salute. "What's rule number two?"

"Well number two isn't a rule, so much as an explanation," she explained. "I'm the N and the S."

"Okay," he intoned slowly before laughing. "What does that mean?"

"It means that there are twelve letters in the words Jumping Jacks, and there were six of us. We each got two letters to spell out the name. I got the N and the S." She liked seeing the amusement glinting in his eyes. "Obviously the best and most important letters in the name," she added, brushing off her shoulders in a mock brag.

She took another deep breath and tried to settle the butterflies in her stomach. The ferocity of his stare was breaking her concentration, so she turned around to have her back facing him. She said she'd show him the cheer, but she didn't say he'd get to see her face during it.

"J-u-m-p-i-n-g j-a-c-k-s!" She whispered the first letters but shouted and launched herself out of the water when she got to the N and S.

"Woo!" he hooted until she turned to glare at him. She waited for him to quiet down with a finger hovering over her lips before she continued the chant.

"We are the Jumping Jacks, and we'll never sit still.

We'll play all day and never get ill.

We'll be together until the end,

Because Jumping Jacks are the very best friends!"

She struck a practiced pose with every beat, keeping her eyes trained on the horizon in a desperate bid to ignore Bennett creeping ever closer behind her. When she finished, she held the final position, one arm behind her head and the other high in the air, much like what every ten-year-old girl imagined a pop star would do.

The cheer released a wave of happy nostalgia and left her invigorated, with its mindless lyrics and simple moves done so often they were second nature. It was a high similar to the ones she experienced after a great ballet performance, although in this instance, the audience was sneaking ever closer to her back instead of sitting demurely in their seats.

The blood coursed through Elana's body, and she was breathing hard, but that wasn't from the cheer. He had come up behind her and was only a few inches away. He didn't touch her with his hands, but every movement sent a pulse of water against her body. It was as intimate as if he had been caressing her entire body himself.

Her shoulder felt the waves of his laughter before it registered in her ears.

"That was great," he said. "Really. I can imagine little Elana dancing around with her cousins and entertaining all the grown-ups at Thanksgiving."

She tried to chuckle but couldn't muster up any more silly energy with his frame so close to hers. Before she had time to do anything, he grabbed her arm and spun her around, mimicking a ballroom dance. One hand slid to hold hers above the water, and the other meandered down her back.

"Five, six, seven, eight," he called loudly, and then took off, pulling her along with him as he attempted skipping turns. She was grateful he was taking over the clown antics because his proximity was beginning to overwhelm her. But instead of relieving the intense sexual tension, his crazy bouncing just transferred all that serious attraction into a more fun and flirty excitement.

They looked absurd spinning around in the middle of the pool and were only making snail-like progress across the water, but she didn't care at all. Her mind could only focus on the smooth rubbing of her body against his as they rebounded off each other in the warm water.

Her stomach slid up and down his abs, and she

could feel the tantalizing outline of his six pack. His board shorts bobbed gently against her thighs, as if they were purposefully taunting her with the promise of what was underneath. So that answered her curiosity about what kind of bathing suit he wore.

She would let him carry her across this pool, just for tonight, because the idea of being anywhere other than cradled in his arms at this moment felt impossible. Every fiber of her being longed to be closer to him.

Bennett was still making jokes about dancing, but Elana could see his mind racing in the same direction as hers. It was as if he wanted to make a move but wasn't going to unless she explicitly consented.

She looked up at the stars, drunk off the vastness of the night sky and the bright full moon. The environment—this house, the pool, even the perfectly calm autumn night—it all lent itself to romance.

Making a decision, she wrapped her arm around the back of his neck and pulled him toward her in a deep kiss. He gave in completely, stopping their bouncing progress and leaving water lapping around their entwined bodies.

It was a good kiss, that's for sure. She had kissed plenty of men, but none with this mix of passion and care. Under the water, his hand gently supported and caressed her lower back. She twisted the small tuft of hair at the back of his neck in response.

When the kiss finally ended, she wasn't sure who had pulled away first. They stayed suspended together, breathing heavily and running their fingers over each other's bodies.

"Bennett, I…" she began, but he silenced her with another kiss. She became weightless as he lifted her up by her hips, allowing her to wrap both legs around his waist as she hadn't done to a man since high school.

She sighed as he slid a hand up and under the back of her bikini top, gently loosening the strings. She was melting into his body with her hands still roving his back when she realized he had stopped and was standing completely still.

For a moment, she thought he regretted what they had been doing, and she cursed the magical twilight that led to yet another mistake. But then she looked at his apologetic eyes staring beyond her. She turned around.

Rose stood in the doorway, towel in hand.

The silence was deafening, and the world, which had so recently been limitless, slammed in to suffocate her. Bennett didn't seem to know what to do.

"Rose, come in," she started, moving sideways across the pool to keep her bikini top from becoming completely untied and hoping Rose hadn't seen much of the make out session. She didn't want the girl to feel uncomfortable in her own home. "Why don't you join us? Your dad told me I could use the pool whenever I wanted, and so I—"

"No, thanks," Rose interrupted, speaking to Elana but never taking her icy eyes off Bennett. She was obviously upset and trying to hold herself together. "You two carry on. Don't worry about me. I'm used to being by myself."

She spun and flew into the house before either of them had a chance to respond. The door clanged loudly behind her, echoing across the open field. Elana was still staring at the empty doorway when Bennett started talking again.

"So look, I should go," he stammered, kneading the

back of his neck where her hand had so recently rested. His fingers flew in aggressive circles, as if he were trying to remove any trace of her contact.

She wasn't sure what to say now. There was nothing to say. "Okay. Of course."

"I don't regret what happened." He motioned vaguely toward her. "I mean, I want that to happen again, if I'm being honest."

"Uh huh." She couldn't trust herself to speak in full sentences. She wanted it to happen again, too. But she didn't know if she should let it. Things were so complicated. Every time she saw him, she started off convinced that she should ignore their attraction, but once he got close, she always seemed to lose her conviction and give in. What did that mean?

"I just need to..." He trailed off as he headed toward the ladder. "I don't know how to put it into words, exactly. I need to figure out how to make all the pieces of my life fit together, if that makes sense."

She nodded as he spoke, trying to follow along. This was the most flustered she had ever seen him, but she couldn't be sure if it was her or Rose who was causing it. Which piece of his life was the most trouble?

"I've caused some problems in the past—taking things too fast, not paying enough attention, that sort of thing. I don't want to do that now. Not with Rose. And not with you."

He grabbed his towel and fled into the house before she could answer, leaving her alone, still bobbing in the water.

She wasn't sure how to take his confession about causing problems in the past and wanting to correct those wrongs. It seemed like a move in the right direction, but at the same time, it brought up how he had treated Rose when she was growing up.

She pushed the negative thoughts down and focused on his encouraging behavior. He was acting like a responsible guy, saying the thing she had been thinking since she found out she was pregnant—that a child should be a parent's first priority. He just wanted to do right by his daughter. Her life was just as messy as his, so she couldn't fault him for having complications. But were both of their lives too chaotic right now to find a way to connect?

She swam slowly to the edge of the pool, any trace of the weightlessness she had felt earlier gone, and lifted herself out. She would concentrate on the positive. She'd deal with the rest tomorrow. This had been a good night, despite the awkward interaction with Rose. She had opened herself up to Bennett, evaluating him as a potential father, and he had said the right things. She smiled and walked leisurely back to her room.

Chapter 5

Sorry about the other night in the pool. Let me make it up to you. Dinner on Friday? Let's get to know each other better. 8:00—B

Elana's hand shook as she read the note again. She knew it by heart but kept rereading obsessively, as if seeing the words would reveal information she had missed. The paper was beginning to crumple on the edges and soften from the nonstop handling, but she couldn't stop herself from fiddling with it.

She had found the note sitting on top of her pillow a few days ago when she returned to her room after another therapeutic swim session. Visits to the pool were becoming a nightly occurrence, although they had all been solo trips since her first run-in with Bennett. Still, the water had a soothing effect, allowing her a place for calm meditation and reflection, and she was starting to come to peace with the baby and her uncertain future.

But that sense of calm had been impossible to find today as dinner with Bennett loomed in the future. She was a bundle of nerves and had spent the afternoon trying on and taking off most of the clothes she had brought with her. In the end, she settled on her favorite red vintage dress and simple gold jewelry. The dress had a boatneck collar and fitted chest that flared out into a circle skirt. She had picked it up at a thrift store with her cousins right before they all went their separate ways after college. That dress always made her feel beautiful.

Even though she was now ready to go, she was still debating whether it was a good idea to have dinner with him. So far, their track record for maintaining self-control around each other was atrocious.

She needed a clear head to figure out the future, and the attraction between them clouded her judgement. Tonight could be the perfect opportunity to explore their connection further, if they were able to ignore their baser instincts. But what did the note mean by *let's get to know each other better*? Would Rose be there, too?

She paused her pacing to stare at the mirror over the desk and check her hair and makeup for the hundredth time. She had to admit, she looked pretty good. All that time spent fiddling with her makeup had paid off. The right side of her hair that never seemed to cooperate was sitting in surprisingly neat waves, and her eyeliner, which she rarely wore outside of performances, was actually symmetrical on both sides. Content, she continued her route around the perimeter of the room. She was amazed her footsteps hadn't yet worn a permanent path in the plush carpeting.

She sighed and tried to imagine how dinner would go but got anxious thinking about it. Building a relationship with a man was hard. Building one with the father of her child was infinitely harder. But trying to piece together a family with two adults who barely knew each other, a teenager who'd just gained a father, and a surprise baby was damn near impossible.

She shook her head and glanced in the ornate

mirror one last time, flicking on a quick coat of light pink lip gloss before heading out the door.

The house was quiet as she walked down the spotless halls, making the sharp clicks of her heels echo ahead. Her body wanted to run forward just to feel the flush that would inevitably come in Bennett's presence, but she kept reminding herself to play it cool. He didn't need to see how desperately she craved his company.

She ran her tongue over her teeth and stretched her mouth wide to loosen up the stiffness that had overtaken her face. She had always been terrible at poker, never able to bluff on even the most low-stakes hands. People could read her face from a mile away. Oh, well. Nothing she could change now.

After smoothing her hair and dress, she took a deep breath and pushed the doors open. She entered with an expectant smile on her face, anticipating the pull of Bennett's eyes, but found only Rose sitting at a large mahogany table already eating a sandwich. The butterflies in her chest churned into a tight ball that dropped down in her gut. She became lightheaded from the abrupt shift to dismay.

"Hi there," she said, hoping Rose couldn't sense her disappointment at Bennett's absence. So that answered one question, at least—Rose would be joining them.

"Hey," Rose answered without looking up. Her eyes were glued to her phone as her thumb constantly flicked up the screen.

Elana looked at the half-eaten sandwich in her hand. "Am I late?"

"For what?"

"For dinner." She sighed. Teenagers always

seemed to speak as little as possible. She wracked her brain trying to remember if she had acted so withdrawn when she was younger and decided she probably had. "Your father asked me to join you guys. I thought he said eight o'clock..." She trailed off as Rose looked up with a confused look.

"I don't know what you're talking about." She shrugged. "He left about an hour ago. Had a date, I think. He asked me whether he was wearing too much cologne."

All the air was sucked out of the room as Rose's words hit her. She melted into a chair at the table and had to gasp for her next breath. "Oh. I must have it wrong, then," she sputtered.

"Guess so." Rose put down her phone and observed Elana with a blank but curious stare. Watching someone be forgotten was apparently the one thing that could pull her away from her screen.

She cursed the fickleness of a teenager's attention span. All she wanted in this moment was to be alone to wallow in self-pity. She couldn't let Rose see her fall apart.

She wasn't sure what exactly to make of Bennett's absence, but it hurt. This was the real him. Despite what he had told her about not having time for romance and focusing on his family, he had another woman he was seeing, maybe more. So what did that make her to him? She was fooling herself when she thought she could be more than a one-night stand. She was just a distraction, a convenient fling he didn't have to leave his house to see. She wasn't even important enough for him to remember a dinner he had invited her to.

She couldn't work through all her emotions right

now, not in front of Rose. She didn't want to color their student/teacher relationship, and besides, her brain was running in all different directions.

"Well, I guess I'll just leave you to your dinner, then." She stood up and started to leave, ready to head back to her room and be alone. "Bye."

"Wait," Rose called after her, interrupting her exit. "We could eat together if you want. There's plenty of sandwich stuff and some leftovers from last night still out in the kitchen."

Elana hesitated, unsure if she could make it through an entire meal right now. With all the thoughts slamming around in her mind, she would barely be able to concentrate on what Rose was saying. But on the other hand, if she went back to her room, she'd have to deal with her emotions. She wasn't sure which was worse.

"You look sad. It's never fun being stood up," Rose cut off her reflections.

Elana flinched at her words, acknowledging their truth immediately. She did feel like she had just been stood up. She had tried to convince herself this wasn't a date, but she had looked forward to this dinner like it was one. She even had perfect hair and a red dress.

"I don't know."

"Aw, come on," Rose pushed, grabbing her by the wrist. It was the first time Rose had touched her, and the kind gesture gave her a glimmer of hope through her confusion. "We could bond over the guy who blew us off. You for dinner and me for my life."

She couldn't turn Rose down after that. Bringing up his abandonment added a fresh layer of anger to her wounds. Now she was enraged not only for herself but for Rose as well. Her nostrils flared as she sat down again.

"I'm sorry you had to grow up without a father," Elana said tenderly, wanting to get that off her chest. She didn't know the right thing to say but figured acknowledging the situation was a good place to start.

"I'm over it." Rose squirmed in her seat and started fidgeting. "I've had longer to come to terms with his jerk moves than you. You'll realize soon enough he only cares about himself."

She was trying to keep a cool demeanor in front of Rose, but the outrage coursing through her veins made her fingers twitch. She opened and closed her hands to release the extra energy. Rose was watching her, eyeing every movement with intense interest, but she still couldn't make herself calm down. She should have known Bennett was trouble and turned down his job offer to tutor Rose. Or better yet, she should have avoided him at the ballet party and dodged all this trouble before their night together.

"I guess," she muttered.

Rose was about to speak but shut her mouth as her face turned white. She looked like she had just seen a ghost.

"You guess what?" a deep voice said in the doorway behind her.

Elana's skin turned cold as she spun around to Bennett beaming at them. His eyes darted between her and Rose, seemingly oblivious to the scene he had interrupted. When no one answered his question, he went on. "I'm glad to see my two favorite ladies are keeping each other company. I want you two to become friends. This place can be isolating if you let it."

Elana didn't know what to say. He was standing there grinning, talking about friendship as if nothing was wrong. She was raging on the inside, ready to hurl all manner of insults, but shouting would show she was emotionally invested in him, and that would be worse than fuming in silence. It would also cause a scene in front of Rose. So instead, she just sneered.

His smile faded as he continued to glance from Elana to Rose. "What is it? Do I have something on my face?"

"Oh, it's nothing," Elana conceded. She crossed her arms and squared her body to him. "I was ready for our dinner, but apparently you forgot. Rose was just stepping in to take your place and keep me company."

His face scrunched into a look of utter confusion. His lips puffed out and his eyes were still darting back and forth between the women. "Forgot what? Our dinner?" When she didn't explain, he faltered and repeated a meager, "What?"

"Don't worry," she said, trying to play it cool but lacing her words with sarcasm. "I figured you had more important things to attend to. I'm just your employee." She emphasized the word employee. "You don't owe me an explanation."

Elana turned to glance at Rose. She was shrinking in her seat and looking out the window, wilting at her father's presence. Her hands were stuffed under her elbows, and she seemed to want to be anywhere but there.

"Rose?" Bennett looked at his daughter, but Elana didn't understand the meaning behind his harsh stare. "I don't know what Elana's talking about, but I have a feeling you do. Can you explain?"

"Don't blame her!" she jumped in, unable to let him criticize Rose. His accusatory words elicited a visceral reaction. How dare he accuse Rose of anything! This was his doing and his alone. Rose needed someone in her corner, and if her father wasn't going to be that person, then she would. "This is between us. You invited me to a dinner, and then you didn't show up for it."

Bennett rubbed his hand through his hair, grimacing, until his face relaxed and he stood up straighter. He looked at Elana and said, "You've got it wrong. I didn't invite you to dinner. But I think Rose might be able to fill us in on what's going on."

She didn't understand his meaning at all, but her eyes followed his as he turned his gaze to Rose, who had almost disappeared under the table.

Without warning, she jerked her body up and glared at him. "Fine!" Rose hissed. "I invited her to dinner."

For a moment, Elana couldn't hear what they were saying as she tried to process this new piece of information. He hadn't stood her up. Rose had invented the whole thing and set her up to feel like she had been abandoned.

"But why?" he asked, softer now.

"I just... You guys are all over each other. It's sickening," Rose started yelling but grew quiet and continued in almost a whisper, "You were together in the pool. I saw you. And every day you practically melt whenever you're in the same room."

"Oh sweetie." He sighed, and his face relaxed. "You don't need to be mad at her. I'm your father. I'll be there for you, no matter what."

"It's not even about her. She's a good teacher." Rose shrugged. It was easy to assume that at sixteen she was more of an adult than a kid, but her vulnerable eyes put her youth on full display. She was a child looking for love from her father. "You're going to leave her anyway. It's what you do."

"Rose, That's not fair." Bennett moved toward her with his arms out in a floundering attempt to hug her, but she stood up and bolted out of the room, leaving a tense silence in her wake.

A few minutes passed before he moved again. Elana wasn't sure whether he remembered that she was there, but she didn't want to disturb him. The scene had been intense, and she was still recovering herself. He was innocent in this situation, but maybe Rose had a point. After all, she had been worrying about him leaving, too. Rose may have gone about it in the wrong way, but her intentions to expose him as a womanizer could have been right. Her hurt from a few minutes before morphed into uncertainty.

He turned back to her, face drooping with exhaustion and sadness. He rubbed his forehead and frowned. "I'm sorry about that. I don't know what else to say."

Elana didn't know what to say, either. "It's okay."

"It's not okay, I know that. But I'm not sure what I'm supposed to do anymore." He took a step toward her and then changed his mind, retreating to a chair in the corner. "I told you she's been having some trouble. Stuff like tonight. I was hoping it would get better after you started working together, but I guess it hasn't."

As she watched his lower lip tremble, she began to soften. His heart appeared to be breaking. She pulled up a heavy chair next to his and sat down, resting her hand on his leg. His muscles loosened as she set her hand down.

She didn't have any advice and couldn't think of anything else to say. She could only listen. "Tell me everything."

The words tumbled out. He told her how Rose had acted out at school, getting herself suspended. Her teachers had thought she was bright but angry. He described the weekly visits to a school-recommended counselor, and how the counselor had reported to him that they had good talks, even though that openness never transferred to him.

Elana listened in silence. She absorbed the information and filed it all away, trying not to leap to conclusions. The details might be valuable later, but in this moment, she needed to hear him out without interrupting. When he finally stopped speaking, his head fell into his hands.

"I can see that you're trying," she said, choosing her words. "Rose will see that eventually, too."

He murmured his assent. "Yeah, I know, I know. But what do I do in the meantime? I'm trying to be her father. I need her to let me."

A response formed on the tip of her tongue, but she wasn't sure if she had the right to say the words. She didn't want to overstep her boundaries.

She started to say, "I don't know," but stopped herself from dodging his question when she saw his pleading eyes urging her on. She would give him her honest opinion, even if that meant offending him. "Did you tell her you're sorry?"

"I told her I know the situation is hard, and I'm

sorry it happened, but we could get through it together."

"Okay, that's a good start, but did you actually say, 'I'm sorry for my part in it'?" She hesitated and then looked straight into his green eyes. "That you're sorry for abandoning her?"

Bennett stiffened and stood up. A wall formed between them once again, but this time, it was him who had built it. She didn't want to anger him, but someone needed to say it. He had abandoned his daughter, and he owed her an apology at the very least.

"But I didn't."

"You didn't what?"

"I didn't abandon her."

It took a moment for her to understand what he was saying. "But Rose said…"

"She lied." His mouth was set in a stern line. He was telling the truth. He was mad, but he wasn't lying. "I didn't abandon my daughter."

Chapter 6

"I didn't abandon Rose," Bennett whispered again, as much to Elana as to himself. He glanced at her wide eyes long enough to see the turmoil but looked away once he started to get drawn in. He couldn't go down that road right now.

His whole body was shaking. Too many thoughts clanged around his mind trying to escape. Rose scared him. He loved her fiercely but was terrified they would never find a way to connect. Plus, he didn't know how to help her with her anger. She was spinning out of control, and he was powerless to stop it.

"What happened?"

He let his head fall back on the carved arch rising high off the back of the chair. He didn't want to talk about it; he was too drained from the earlier confrontation with Rose, not to mention the previous months of living in a constant state of tension.

He thought briefly about deflecting Elana's question but decided against it. He needed to tell her everything now, before she had a chance to form her own opinion, or at least before her current opinion of him could get any worse. He didn't want her to believe Rose's lie any longer than she already had. And if he took a few days to explain himself, she might think he was taking the time to make up a story.

Without lifting his head off the chair, he spoke. "I

don't know what Rose told you about the past or her childhood, but I didn't know I had a daughter until a few months ago."

After a beat of silence, he turned toward her, trying to gauge her response to his admission.

Her eyes widened, pleading with him to keep talking and explain, but the words were slow to form. Since meeting Rose, he hadn't told anyone the full truth about their history. He'd been in too much shock to give his father a full explanation in the beginning, and by the time he was ready to talk, his father didn't have the patience to hear his side of the story, preferring to write him off as the screw up of the family. He was used to the treatment and hadn't bothered to argue, instead giving in to his father's ultimatum to babysit the house for his brother. And because of his seclusion in this mansion stuck out in the middle of nowhere, barely any of his friends knew he had a daughter. He needed to start talking to someone, even if only to practice the explanation he'd give everyone else. People would start asking questions eventually, and he needed to be able to answer them.

"Rose's mother and I dated in college. It wasn't serious, only a few months. There were some good times, but we never got to the 'I love you' stage. We were headed in different directions, so we broke up after graduation and each went our separate ways. I haven't seen her in years." He took a deep breath before finishing the story. "She never told me she was pregnant."

"Then how did you find out about Rose?" Her question was eager, although gentler than before, more understanding.

"Rose showed up at my doorstep with a suitcase and letter from a lawyer a few months ago. The letter granted me full parental rights. That was it. Her mother is gone, so she only has me." He shrugged, sighing. "We only have each other, I guess. I had a really rough time getting used to the idea in the beginning, but I'm head over heels for the kid now and don't know what I'd do without her. Unfortunately, Rose has been much slower to come around, and she's obviously still furious about the situation."

He glanced at her. She was slowly nodding. Telling her about how Rose came to stay with him had been easier than anticipated. She made him feel comfortable.

They sat together in silence, each working down a different path in their thoughts. Elana was the first to speak.

"Okay," she said slowly, choosing her words. "Then why did she tell me you abandoned her?"

His heart sank. If Rose was telling people he had abandoned her, then she was still as angry at him as the first day she'd arrived. He had been telling himself they were making progress, but obviously they weren't. He'd been struggling with guilt over his absence from Rose's childhood for months, and he couldn't seem to escape it. His logical side understood he hadn't abandoned her, but his emotional side only felt the acute pain of missing sixteen years of his daughter's life.

"I don't really know. Like I told you before, she's been lying about stuff. Telling people things about her past that aren't real. It's gotten her in trouble in school. I think the whole thing with her mom really messed her up, and she's taking it out on me."

"All of that is incredibly difficult for a kid. I guess it makes sense she'd lie," Elana admitted. "Things must have been hard for her all those years. Growing up without her father and then suddenly having him back in her life."

With her words, a thought dawned on him for the first time, and he gasped, leaning his head back and closing his eyes in order to stop himself from crying. "What if Rose doesn't believe me? That I never knew about her, I mean." He pushed back the tears that threatened to appear. "She may actually believe I abandoned her. It may not have been a lie to her."

He stood up suddenly, his chair scratching on the ground. He started pacing, head in his hands. "I'm trying so hard to make the past right, but what if she'll never let me get beyond it? It could haunt me forever."

He stopped and looked straight into Elana's uncertain eyes.

"I'm sure she believes you," she stammered, breaking eye contact and looking down at her twisting hands.

"Come on, tell me the truth," he begged, reaching out to her. He was completely vulnerable now, and there was no turning back. "I trust you. I don't know why, but I do. I trust you implicitly. So please, tell me the truth."

"Maybe…" Elana hesitated as if she wasn't sure she should continue, but he couldn't let her stop now.

He squatted in front of her chair so their eyes were at the same level. "What?" he said gently, placing his hands on hers to stop their anxious movements. "You can tell me. I can take it."

"Well, it's just that maybe it doesn't matter if Rose

believes you."

He stared blankly at her. He didn't know what she was talking about.

"I mean, it matters to you, of course, but what if you can't change it on her end? What if you can't make her believe you?" She was leaning forward earnestly, so close he wanted to lean his forehead against hers. "I can see it's important to you that she believe you, but it's also possible she might never. This doesn't seem like something you can prove. It's just your word against whatever story she heard growing up."

The truth of her words shone through beneath their initial sting. She was right. Rose may never believe he'd been in the dark about her existence. There was no way to know what information she had been given for the past sixteen years. He might always be the man who abandoned her. But if that was true, what could he do to salvage their relationship?

"I know," he agreed, nodding slowly.

"And that's hard for you, and yes, definitely unfair," she continued, scooting closer toward the edge of her seat. "But if you accept that, you can move forward. Improve the future instead of focusing on the past."

The pain of his realization was starting to dissipate, and Bennett sensed a light at the end of the tunnel. "You're right," he conceded. "It might be that way now, but maybe not forever. I need to give up on trying to convince her of my innocence in the past and instead focus on building trust today."

He pulled her forward into a hug and leaned his head in her hair. He was trying to blink back tears, only this time, they were tears filled with hope. She was raising him out of the rut of self-pity he had fallen into over the past few weeks. Every time he was in her presence, she helped him see a way forward. She empowered him to push farther and think fully about the future.

"I need to accept that Rose is the only one who can forgive me for not being there during her childhood. And I can't control her forgiveness. Can't make it come any faster. I can only control my own actions in the present, and I'm going to make her love the person I am today."

"That sounds like a good plan."

She squeezed his hands as he continued forcefully, high off the adrenaline now racing through his body. "No, not the person I am today...the father I am today."

He sat forward in his chair, breathless. A tremendous weight had been lifted, and the lightness was dizzying.

"Come on, let's walk." He straightened up and tugged on her hand.

She hesitated, but stood and looped her arm through his. A comforting warmth crept toward his shoulder as her arm settled against his. He felt like they'd known each other for years.

"Look, we can talk about this more later," he said. "You know the basics of my complicated past for now, at least. And you've already helped me see things more clearly. Let's go out and get some fresh air."

"Sure." She was rubbing her bottom lip with her free hand absentmindedly, and Bennett watched her finger slide smoothly back and forth.

It looked like she believed him, but he couldn't be sure. The defensiveness and anger she had displayed earlier were gone, replaced with a more open demeanor.

Elana was the first person he had really talked to about Rose, other than lawyers. He had been alone in this struggle for months. Now, he had a confidant and a potential ally.

****

After Bennett pulled her up, they kept walking arm in arm. Neither acknowledged the gesture; they simply walked while still linked, as if it were the most natural thing in the world. She wrapped her hand around his, their fingers intertwining, and a tingling pulse penetrated the skin of her palm where each of his fingers rested. Her thumb stroked his hand automatically in response.

Her image of him as a jerk playboy was being torn down and replaced with a new one. He was a man struggling to do the best he could in a difficult situation. These two conflicting ideas wavered back and forth in her mind as they meandered through the grand hallways in comfortable silence.

The antique frames and artwork glided past them in a string of color, although she couldn't focus on any single piece. She was following the pathways of her mind and wandering through the house without a destination. She was floating with him, driven by pure inertia, and would follow wherever he led.

Finally, she decided the only thing to do was listen to her heart, which ached from the distress she saw in his eyes as he spoke about Rose, and her body, which was currently buzzing from the closeness they shared. She trusted him deep in her core, despite all the conflicts in her head. That had to mean something.

Bennett paused at the door to the deck, looking out

at the pool with a twinkle in his eye. As she noticed what he was eyeing, he raised his eyebrows twice in quick succession, a goofy gesture that enticed a smile onto her lips. He chuckled in response. The unexpected release lifted the last bits of tension from their stressful talk.

As the air vibrated from his laughter, she became aware of just how close their bodies had become. Every inch of her stood at attention from the proximity, and she had to fight the tantalizing pull of her skin toward his. The tension sent a shiver down her stomach that ended between her thighs.

That had been happening a lot recently. In addition to the waves of nausea and exhaustion, her libido was in overdrive. Something about the pregnancy hormones made the slightest touch, even from a gentle wind, wake her body up in novel ways. It was both frustrating and exhilarating. The increased sensations snuck up on her at inopportune moments, distracting from her work and clouding her judgement about Bennett, but also leading to some intense solo moments she definitely enjoyed. She considered that to be one of the only perks of pregnancy so far.

Her mind was emboldened by the eagerness of her body. He had shared his deepest emotions, told her the entire truth of his complex history. He had his faults, of course, but he was also a good man. A good man in need of someone who believed him and supported him. She could be there for him without betraying Rose, couldn't she?

She decided to stop debating and act. She cupped her hands around his chin, taking pleasure in the soft scratchiness of the five o'clock shadow framing his face. He muttered, a low, throaty sound, and she pulled him gently toward her. When their lips met, it was as if she had unlocked a part of him he had been holding back, and his arms immediately snapped around her.

What had begun as a gentle caress quickly turned into an urgent embrace. Bennett held one hand behind her neck to keep their lips firmly pressed together, while the other roved down her back.

Her eyes closed as she let out an indistinct moan. Her head started swimming, and the only things she could make out were their tongues wrestling for mooring as their hands trespassed into previously forbidden territory.

He pulled back but didn't release her face, instead staring into her eyes with a hunger that made her struggle to catch her breath and practically drool with anticipation.

"Are you sure about this?" he asked, chewing at his lip. "Once I start, I won't be able to stop."

"Then don't," she whispered.

That was all it took. His lips were back on hers before she could fully inhale. His hands slowly followed the curve of her body down her arms, around her back, and over the outline of her backside, sending a wave of pleasure down to her toes. She gasped when he suddenly seized under her thighs to pick her up and carry her through the next door to one of the sumptuous sofas in the entertainment room. She wrapped her legs around his body to hold on and appreciated the stiffness of his desire pressed against her.

The force of his sweeping movement sent chills down her spine. The hot air of his breath, heavier now than before, lapped against her exposed shoulders and back, while twirls of air lifted her dress beyond the reach of his hands with each step. She became keenly aware of each new inch of skin revealed, and so, it seemed, did he.

As he set her down, he kneeled in front of her, sliding her legs apart and positioning himself between them. She watched him take a slow, deep breath as he looked her up and down.

"You're truly a stunning woman," he said, his eyes on hers, while his hands slid her dress upward. "I've been looking at you for weeks. Now, I'm going to taste you."

Her core contracted in response to his words. She started to sit up but stopped as he held up a hand.

"Lean back," he huffed. "I told you, I'm going to taste you, and I want to try all of you."

As he spoke, his fingers reached their destination between her legs and began a light stroke, teasing the upcoming event. The delicate touch sent a quiver through Elana's body and up to her cheeks. She inched toward him, begging for more pressure. It was clear that the fireworks they'd experienced during their first night together weren't a fluke.

He slid her panties down with his free hand, maintaining his tormenting touch. It made her squirm with anticipation.

If he was going to play with her eagerness, then she could do the same back to him. She let one of her hands distractedly caress her stomach, baiting him with the show. She smiled at his eyes hungrily watching it. Her hand travelled up to her breast and began slowly circling. When her fingers finally reached her nipple and gave it a gentle pull, he groaned and practically dove between her legs.

The intensity of his tongue caused her to arch her back to fully meet him. His mouth continued its conquest, while his hand explored the length of her legs and the line of her stomach. Shudders of pleasure jolted her core, with each surge strengthening beyond the previous one.

As if he could read exactly what her body craved, he reached one hand between her legs and flicked her most sensitive spot at the crest of one wave, never letting go with his mouth. The dual sensations pushed her over the edge into a powerful orgasm that shook her entire frame.

When he released her, she jerked toward him reflexively. That orgasm had been amazing, but it wasn't enough. Her body was primed, and she wanted more.

As he stood up above her, hunger burned in his eyes. She maintained eye contact while reaching out to grab the swell in his pants. His erection grew harder under her grasp.

"My turn," Elana purred, standing up without letting go. She watched his eyes harden, but all it took was a raised eyebrow to make him surrender. The power gave her a heady rush.

"Lay down over there."

She nodded toward the sofa behind her, making Bennett whirl around. Their eyes locked, and she could feel his pulse quickening as they lowered onto the cushions together.

Without breaking eye contact, she swung one leg over his hips and gently slid him inside her. She began a slow rocking, enjoying the full length of his erection.

She wanted to draw this out as long as possible.

She watched as his eyes pleaded, and relished his hands exploring her body in ever more frantic motions. When they were both on the verge of coming, he suddenly reached one hand behind her back and the other behind her bottom. He picked her up and spun her around so he could reach her deepest places.

She gasped involuntarily at the abrupt change in position and was immediately plunged into an extended orgasm that made her lightheaded.

They were both panting hard when they finally rolled apart, disengaging themselves slowly from the tight clasp. Bennett had a goofy grin on his face she had never seen before. He looked almost giddy.

"What?" She giggled, catching his infectious happiness.

"Oh nothing." The edges of his lip curled into a smirk, and he had a devious look in his eye. "I was just thinking about how much I'm going to enjoy making you come again."

His brashness shocked her, but she didn't have long to think about it as he pitched back toward her and kissed her hard. This was going to be a long night.

Chapter 7

Bennett had already been awake for half an hour when the morning light bounced off the stainless-steel coffee pot in the corner directly into his eye. He was lying perfectly still on the couch so he wouldn't wake Elana, who was sleeping crammed in beside him. The small blanket they shared covered only her sloping backside, and he was enjoying examining her exposed curves. But this damn sun in his eye made that impossible. He swore silently and began the slow process of untangling from their embrace.

The entirety of the previous night felt like a dream. It had started off terribly with his fight with Rose, but ended in a surreal and seemingly endless night of passion. He wasn't sure what either of those things meant, but he knew they were in conflict with each other.

Elana was quickly becoming an undeniable force in his life. Every time she was near him, he craved her touch. But that was proving to be an obstacle in his relationship with Rose, who had made it clear she didn't think she could rely on him. And if she couldn't trust him, how could she love him as her father?

Finally free from the tangle of limbs, he tiptoed to the glimmering coffee pot in the corner. His father kept the entertainment room fully stocked with every drink and snack item a person could want, despite guests rarely coming into the only informal room in the house.

Elana sighed as she rolled over and peeked out at him through squinted blue eyes. She looked around, assessing the room and trying to get her bearings. "What time is it?"

He glanced at the bright red numbers on the coffee pot. "Just turned seven. Go back to sleep. You don't need to wake up just because I am. I've always been an early bird. Getting that worm and whatnot."

"No, I'm getting up," she mumbled, burying her face back in the fluffy pillow. The way she still laid half uncovered and completely vulnerable made him think she hadn't fully woken up when she spoke to him. Her body draped unselfconsciously off the side of the couch and around the blanket, reminding him of the many ways they had both given in to passion last night.

He smiled and grabbed his coffee mug, letting its warmth heat his hand until he could no longer take it. He headed toward a nook in the corner, ready to spend a lazy morning reading, drinking coffee, and watching her sleep. As he sank onto the plush pillows, the bench beneath him let out a loud groan. At the noise, Elana popped up from the couch, startled. She squinted at him through the one eye not covered by her messy bed-head hair and cleared her throat.

"Dammit," he muttered softly under his breath. Then he raised his voice to say, "Sorry."

"It's okay," she said. "If you had wanted me to wake up, you could have just come back over here and—"

"No, I didn't mean to," he interrupted her before she could go on. He knew some of the ways he could have woken her up, and most made him blush to imagine, but if they started down that path now, they'd be stuck in this room all day. And he couldn't chance Rose walking in on them in another compromising position. Not until he had a chance to talk to her about Elana and smooth things over from last night.

"What are you up to today?" Elana wandered across the room toward him, toes dragging on the velvety rug, leaving long strokes in her wake. She ran her fingers over everything, examining all the shelves and making him see the room through her eyes. He had grown up angry at the isolation and even more furious at his parents for choosing to live here, so he never truly appreciated the beauty of the historic home. Even though he could see she was impressed, he was still hit by a teenage embarrassment as he noticed the high number of video games he owned.

He had to think fast. She was heading his way, and if she got much closer and ran her fingers over him, his willpower to leave would crumble.

"What about a drive?"

"A drive?" She stopped and raised her eyebrows. It was clearly not the response she had been expecting.

"Yeah, the mountains around here are beautiful, especially in the morning when there's smoke rising off the peaks. You haven't really gotten a proper look yet, have you?"

"Well, no. I guess not."

"So then let's go. You're a city girl, and I bet you can't see too many mountains when you're walking around the busy streets of DC." He sounded too eager. He needed to play it cool. "I mean, there's nothing like riding the curves of a mountain road in an expensive car."

She chuckled. The mention of his luxury car was too much. He was turning into the stereotype of a rich playboy that his brother, Chance, had perfected. But it seemed to amuse her. He'd play the cheesiness up, then. Anything to hear more of her laugh.

"Don't laugh," he scolded, squinting his eyes and smirking. "Let me impress you. I want you to feel the power under you. Enjoy the ride, baby." He winked and put on his best schmoozy grin.

It pushed her over the top, and she fell onto the bench next to him, her small giggle turning into a big, hooting laugh. He had done it—completely disarmed her and gotten another glimpse of the carefree woman she kept guarded. It felt so good to make her happy that he almost gave in and snuggled up to her. But he wouldn't. He wanted to learn more about who this woman was, and he knew they wouldn't be talking if they stayed there.

"Come on." He grabbed her hand and pulled her off the cushions so hard she hopped slightly in the air. "I wasn't kidding about you needing to feel the power."

****

Elana had never paid much attention to what model car she drove and silently judged people riding around in expensive sports cars, but this vehicle demanded that she sit up and take notice. Each swooping curve and rev of the engine gave her a thrill, and she enjoyed imagining the view of the car's brilliant yellow profile standing in stark contrast to the verdant landscape.

Colors streaked past, and the trees blended together in her mind. She cracked the window to feel the wind blow through her hair, not caring about how disheveled she'd look when they would finally stop. The sharp air made her feel more awake than she had in a long time, and she was suddenly a little regretful she had spent so many days of her life closed in a dance studio. A whole big world existed that she hadn't yet explored.

For the first time, being fired from the ballet seemed like it could have an upside. She now had the freedom to do things that weren't allowed in the strict lifestyle of a professional dancer. She could go on extended vacations, eat any food she wanted, and do extreme sports like skiing that carried a high risk of injury. Or she could just be in the mountains, enjoying the crisp autumn air with a new beau who made her heart leap. Maybe life after the stage wouldn't be so bad.

The road wound through the lush countryside over gentle rolling hills, creating the false impression from afar that a drive between the mountains would be predictable. In fact, the curves and slope of the road combined to create hairpin turns that made her stomach jump into her throat. And Bennett relished every chance to impress her. He was doing his best imitation of a professional racecar driver, shifting dramatically before turns, revving the engine, and generally delighting in making her grip the handle above the door for stability. She didn't usually find macho behavior appealing, but he was so damn excited about showing off for her that she couldn't help but be attracted to him.

"We've got two more big curves up ahead, and then the road calms down a bit," he called over the deep bellow of the engine. "Think you can handle it?"

She nodded, ready to steady herself on the door. In truth, the curves were starting to get to her. The increased G forces took a toll on her tired body, and she wasn't feeling great. A gentle section of road would come as a welcome break. Of course, she couldn't let him know that.

"Bring it on."

The car roared through two more turns, Bennett shifting with ferocity in an apparent attempt to push the car to its limit for one final performance. With each downshift, the knot in her stomach grew, and she had to work to hide her relief at the sight of a straight stretch of road before them.

"What did you think?" he asked, grinning from ear to ear like a kid in a school play.

"Very impressive," she relented. "You're right. That was unlike any car ride I've experienced before."

"I'm glad."

They rode in a comfortable silence for a few minutes, and Elana enjoyed being near him without needing to speak.

Finally, he broke the stillness. "Do you know where we are?"

"Other than in the mountains, not really," she admitted.

"We basically made a big loop. We headed away from the house going north, circled down south through the mountains, and are now heading back up toward the house. We went around the town, so it's probably different from the way you drove in." Bennett pointed to a field up ahead, bordered by a long wooden fence. It was the first sign of human civilization she had seen in a while.

"That's the beginning of Wakefield land. We have stables down here and a small guesthouse farther on. My brothers and I used to go riding almost every day when we all still lived here. One of us won the local rodeo most years we competed. It was usually Peter, although I gave him a run for his money the year he was distracted with the SATs. He was always really connected to the horses."

She was glad to hear him sharing a happy memory about his family instead of the usual serious stories. Family was important; she couldn't imagine life without her mom and cousins. And once everyone grew up and went their separate ways, memories helped keep that love alive.

"Now there's a stable hand from town who looks after the horses most of the time, since it's only Rose and I here, and she hasn't shown any interest in learning to ride." He was talking and gesturing out the window. "Hey, I have an idea." His face brightened. "I'll bet the horses are lonely and would enjoy some exercise. Do you want to go for a ride?"

"A ride on a horse?" she questioned, although she knew very well that's what he was suggesting. She had never ridden a horse before. It had always been deemed too dangerous, the risk of injury too great.

"Well, yeah," he replied, shaking his head.

She was scared, but she was also feeling somewhat inspired by the drive here and her newfound resolve to go outside her comfort zone to try different things.

"Okay," she decided. If she could perform on stage, she could certainly ride a horse. It would be easy. At least, that's what she kept telling herself.

Chapter 8

Bennett turned left at the next gravelly road and guided the car slowly over each bump. Elana opened her mouth to make fun of him for babying his car but got distracted as she caught sight of a towering, red barn next to a field. Giant doors with white, crisscrossed beams marked the entrance to the barn, and several paddocks stood behind it, emptying into large fields that extended into the mountainside. The image could have been lifted straight from the pages of a magazine.

She had to keep reminding herself that this mansion, with its never-ending supply of beautiful buildings and scenery, was actually his house. She had never known anyone with as much family money before, and it still took some getting used to.

They parked in a clearing next to the closest paddock, and he led her up through the huge barn doors.

"Right now, there are only four horses in the stable," he was saying. "There's room for twelve, but we don't keep that many anymore. Not enough people to ride them. Now we just have them for guests and the annual fair. It's a shame, really, because they love to be around people."

She watched him walk from stall to stall, greeting each horse by name and petting each one. His hand dove into a feed bag at the end of the row, and he pulled out a few carrots that he slipped into his pockets for later. He seemed to forget about her for a moment and focused solely on the horses. He obviously cared deeply for these animals and shared a special connection with them.

"Which one calls out to you?" he asked, turning back to her after he had attended to each horse. "They're all great, but I've learned that people generally feel a connection to a particular animal, and it's best to follow that instinct."

"I don't know. This one, maybe?" She stepped up to the horse in the closest stall.

"No. Take your time," he cooed, putting his arm around her shoulder and gesturing toward the horses. "Take a moment to look at each and see if you prefer one. I guarantee the ride will be easier with the right horse."

She breathed out and looked around slowly, finally locking eyes with a small dappled horse in the last stall. Its gray and white spots were mesmerizing, but she was really drawn in by its kind brown eyes. Plus, it looked the least intimidating of the horses.

"That one." She pointed at the horse.

"Ah, that's Bolt." He smiled and led her toward the stall, placing a carrot in her free hand. "We named her before we realized she was more of a looker than a racer. She can go fast if she needs to, but she prefers to saunter through the fields enjoying nature. Says hello to any rabbit she crosses paths with. She would be my top choice for you to ride as a first timer."

"Hey! How can you tell I'm a first timer?" she cried, feigning offense.

"Well," he said, sidling up to her and leading her toward Bolt. "No reason, exactly. Except you haven't gone anywhere near the horses since we walked in. You have been doing an excellent job of helping me hold up the wall, though."

She laughed in spite of herself. He was right. She had been frozen to a spot against the beams on the far side of the barn while he had greeted all the horses so naturally.

"Bolt sounds perfect to me, then. I trust you." She shocked herself with her mention of trust. She hadn't said it out loud before, but it was true. She trusted him to protect her around these horses, and that allowed her to act brave.

She walked the last few feet to Bolt by herself and placed her hand near the horse's mouth. Bolt responded gently, nibbling at the carrot and tilting her head toward Elana as if asking to be pet.

"Hi, girl," she whispered, stroking the side of her head. "My name's Elana. Nice to meet you."

She sensed Bennett behind her. His hand ran the length of her arm until it rested on hers.

"She likes to be touched like this."

He guided her hand around Bolt's strong face. She appreciated the way their arms rested together and how his chest melted into her back. His warmth radiated through her core and to her toes.

"You keep doing this, and I'll saddle up our horses." He tapped her on the shoulders and walked to the back of the barn where lots of mysterious leather gear she couldn't identify hung on the wall. He grabbed a few things and headed back over to Bolt. He laid a blanket on the horse's back and smoothed it before placing the saddle on top. He let the smooth leather straps hang down and then cinched them tight. Elana was amazed at how quickly his hands worked. The movements were clearly second nature to him, like tying up pointe shoes was to her.

He walked to another horse and repeated the process while she refocused her attention on Bolt.

"It's you and me girl," she whispered. "Please be nice. I'd really appreciate it."

Her stomach grumbled as she talked, and she rubbed it hard to try and quiet it. She was getting hungry. Skipping breakfast wasn't a very good idea. Hopefully the ride would be fairly quick, and they could grab some lunch after.

"One final touch."

Elana jumped as he spoke into her ear. How was he able to sneak up on her so well?

She spun around. He stood with his arms held out, a hat in one hand and cowboy boots in the other. A wide brimmed leather cowboy hat rested on his head, throwing a mysterious shade across his eyes. The scene sent a little thrill through her body.

"You want me to dress like a cowboy?" she asked incredulously.

"Yep. Well, cowgirl, actually." He was grinning from ear to ear, obviously pleased with his plan.

Her eyes scanned down his legs. He was already sporting his own pair of well-worn cowboy boots.

"It's the uniform here. We keep extras in the closet for newbies like you who don't come prepared."

Transforming into a cowgirl was not what she had planned, although she didn't mind watching him play cowboy. She continued staring with her eyebrows raised.

"Plus, it'll make your riding experience safer," he added seriously after a beat of silence, raising the boots and hat higher.

That made her relent. She couldn't argue with safety. "Okay, fine." She grabbed the hat and boots out of his hands and slipped them on. Everything fit perfectly. She stepped forward and did a little skip in the air, clicking her heels together on one side like a cowboy in a musical. She held onto a pretend belt buckle and sauntered over to him. "Hey there, partner," she drawled.

He touched the brim of his hat, tipping it forward slightly in greeting. "Ma'am." He winked and then gestured toward the horses. "Are you ready for this?"

Nervousness overshadowed her goofy mood. In her joking about being a cowgirl, she had almost forgotten about the horseback riding. She thought for a brief moment about changing her mind but then decided she wasn't a coward. She could do this. She swallowed hard and walked toward Bolt, all the time wondering how on earth she'd get up on that saddle.

****

Bennett wiped the sweat from his forehead and rubbed it across his jeans. It was suddenly hot in the barn, and that wasn't just the weather. He watched Elana striding up to Bolt, her tight jeans and swaying shirt amplifying her figure. She was clearly out of her element, but he admired her courage to keep moving forward and try something new.

She was standing at Bolt, gripping the saddle in different ways and trying to hop one leg over her back. She'd never get up on the horse that way.

"I'm coming," he called, jogging over and placing his hands on her hips. "On the count of three, I'll lift you up, and you swing your leg over."

"Okay."

"One…two…three!" He lifted her up and over the horse, giving a firm push on her backside as she brought her leg over the saddle. "There you go." He helped her slip each foot into a stirrup as she adjusted her weight in the saddle, and then placed a rein in each hand.

"Bolt is a good horse. You don't have to yank or pull hard on the reins. No sudden movements. She'll just follow Ares, my horse, and she'll respond to a light tug on the reins if you want her to stop."

"Okay," she responded again. She was much less talkative than before, and her mouth was set in a hard line. Tension radiated from her entire body.

"Hey!" He slapped her thigh gently, forcing her to break her distant stare and look him in the eyes. She jumped at his touch. "Relax, please. You're making me nervous."

She gave him a small smile, but her eyes were still worried. He walked across the barn and hopped onto his horse. When he was settled, he nudged his feet into Ares' sides and ambled out into the corral. He turned to watch Bolt following behind with Elana on her back.

"We'll just stay in the corral for now," he said to her. "Until you feel comfortable."

"Mmhmm."

She gave a barely perceptible nod in response to his words while staring straight ahead with laser-like focus. He had to admire her for facing her fears. Not everyone would be so willing to do that.

He trotted Ares around in a circle for a few minutes with Bolt close behind, to let her get used to the feel of riding, and then decided she might be comfortable enough to have a conversation. He wanted to talk and get to know her. To listen to what she had to say and learn more about who she was.

"So how has it been staying here the past month?" he began, thinking her time at his estate would be a good place to start.

"Rose is great. She—"

But he cut her off, not wanting to talk about Rose. It seemed like they only ever talked about his daughter. She was his world, of course, but he wanted to know about Elana herself.

"I mean," he said deliberately, "how has it been for you? Have you enjoyed working here?"

"Oh," she said, eyebrows raising. "It's been pretty wonderful, actually. I'll admit that I was nervous about coming to live at your house at first. Especially with our past."

A flush crept across her cheeks at the mention of their shared history, and he felt that heat reflected in his own face. He watched her eyes twinkling in the sunlight and her hair flowing in the wind as she bounced up and down on the horse, and his pants tightened. He looked away to the mountains behind her to clear his mind.

"Well I'm glad you came," he stammered, trying to regain his composure. "I think it's worked out pretty well."

"It has," she agreed cheerfully.

"Tell me more about your life in DC. What do you do there, aside from ballet?"

He had asked these questions of women before but

had never cared about the answers, not really. They had just been part of the dance that was dating. With Elana, though, he really wanted to know. He wanted to be able to paint a complete picture of her in his head.

"There's not much mystery." She shrugged. "Dancers don't have any free time. I'm no exception."

"But when you do get a day off...?" he urged her on. "Unless you want me to guess?"

"No, no. Okay." She thought for a moment, looking at the reins in her hands. "I spend most of my time with my mom. We go to a farmer's market every weekend and try to see at least one play a month. I love anything theatrical, which is not surprising given how much time I spend on a stage."

"Makes sense."

He enjoyed hearing her talk. Her words had a musical quality, probably from years immersed in a world of rhythm.

He was about to ask her more about her daily life, find out where she had her coffee or went to blow off steam, but then her face contorted into a grimace.

"I need to get down!" she cried. The urgency in her voice made him spring into action. He practically flew off Ares and ran over to her, grabbing Bolt's reins in one hand and sweeping her off the horse with the other in a single motion. All the color had drained from her face, and she looked like she was about to pass out. Something was clearly wrong.

****

Elana was embarrassed at her sudden outburst, but the mild hunger she felt earlier had grown into a gentle queasiness while rocking back and forth on the horse's back. Then nausea had hit full force. Skipping breakfast and driving through the winding countryside at high speeds had definitely been a bad decision. Her head was swimming, and her stomach was screaming an all too familiar warning.

"Excuse me," she blurted quickly once her feet hit the dirt. She didn't want to throw up in front of Bennett. She fumbled her way past him, getting tangled in the loose reins, and ran full speed toward the corral door, hoping to make it behind a wall before she got sick. But it was too late. She only managed to hide herself behind a small trough at the perimeter of the paddock.

He rushed over to her side and stood gently stroking her back. He stayed quietly next to her until she was able to stand up.

"Are you okay?"

She nodded but couldn't meet his eyes. Her cheeks burned with humiliation. This certainly ranked up there as one of her most mortifying moments.

"I'm okay now. I think I just need to eat something. I should've had breakfast," she mumbled. She hesitated, about to tell him about the pregnancy. She felt guilty about keeping it from him but still wasn't sure what she wanted. What would she ask of him? No, she couldn't tell him about the baby until she knew what her expectations of him would be. Then she remembered Rose and all the trouble he was having bonding with her. This was definitely not the right time.

She didn't want him to become suspicious at her sudden bout of nausea, so she quickly added, "Sometimes I get sick if I go too long without eating. Low blood sugar."

At the mention of food, Bennett snapped into action. "Ah, of course. I should have thought of that."

He slapped his forehead while gently urging her toward the car with his other hand. "We're right by the guest cottage on the edge of the property. That has a fully stocked kitchen because the stable hand sometimes stays there on the weekend. I'll make you something."

She wasn't surprised that there was a fully stocked kitchen nearby. Every part of the Wakefield estate came equipped with whatever a guest might need. Staying with Bennett was better than staying in a four-star hotel.

He helped her ease back into the car and closed the door behind her. She watched as he ran around the hood to get in as quickly as possible. Even through her embarrassment and upset stomach, she had to smile at his boyish eagerness. His wide eyes revealed the depths of his concern and his uncertainty about her health. Guilt slammed into her. She had ruined this perfect day.

"You don't need to make a fuss," she insisted. "I'm really okay."

"I know you are."

She nodded and decided not to mention how cautiously he was now driving compared to earlier. He didn't speed around bends or shift like a madman this time.

"Let's just go get you food anyway," he added.

She leaned her head back and took a deep breath while he slid his hand onto her thigh. His kind touch held all the electricity of their passionate encounter from the night before, except this time, it was also filled with worry. She glanced at him out of the corner of her eye. His body radiated determination as he sat up straight with his mouth set in a tight line. He was in full-on protector mode, and testosterone was oozing off him as he became a man with a purpose. He was going to get her food. And she would let him take care of her.

As they drove toward the guest cottage, she wondered idly what kind of beautiful house this would be, and whether it had as many comfy sofas as the main house.

Chapter 9

Bennett flew around the clean, modern kitchen in the guest house, grabbing pans from below the counter and pulling food out of the fridge.

While the main house was all classic mahogany and deep velvets, the guest cottage was sleek minimalist and designed for function. Immense white cabinets filled an entire wall, and stainless steel adorned every handle and appliance. White marble countertops overflowed into a waterfall edge that made the kitchen island blend seamlessly into the floor, and a row of geometric hanging lights added intrigue to the otherwise horizontal lines of the room. The entire scene was bathed in light from floor to ceiling windows designed to maximize the afternoon sun. It was as if a chic New York loft had been dropped into the mountains.

Elana was cleaning herself up in the bathroom, and he wanted to have eggs and toast cooked for her before she came out. His spirits were high, because despite her illness, they were having a great day. Ever since telling her the truth about Rose, the blockade between them had been torn down. He was able to envision a relationship between the two of them and not just a fling. He couldn't deny the attraction on a purely physical level, but more than that, Elana was one of the smartest and strongest women he had ever met. Plus, the conversation flowed between them more naturally than it ever had with another woman. This could be something real, if he could find a way to make it fit with Rose.

He shredded a block of sharp cheddar, assuming everyone liked a good cheese omelet. He hoped she was feeling better, and he was going to do his best to take care of her. His optimism about their relationship made the whole world seem bright, and he wanted her to view it the same way.

"If you need anything, check under the sink," he shouted toward the bathroom. "There's lots of random stuff in there."

She murmured something unrecognizable in assent, so he went back to the loud business of finding the pan he wanted. For a rarely used guest house, this place sure had a lot of extra junk.

A few minutes later, the bathroom door opened, and Elana's soft footsteps came down the hall. He turned to see her glide into the room. Even when she wasn't feeling well, she still floated along the floor as if she were dancing. Her hair was disheveled in a messy bun with little tendrils escaping. The disarray chipped away at her usually polished exterior, and he was overcome by a strong urge to embrace her.

She stopped just past the doorway, posed midway in her stride, and he realized he was staring.

"How are you feeling?" he stuttered, shaking his head and refocusing on the omelets. The air behind the stove suddenly became stifling.

"I'm better, thanks." She walked toward the kitchen and leaned on the back of a barstool, sniffing at the air. "That smells fancy. Who knew you were such a good cook?"

"I'm not actually. This is just a plain cheese omelet." He smirked and lowered his voice to a whisper, motioning for her to come closer. She leaned in, near enough that he could smell the fresh scent of lavender soap diffusing from her skin. "My grandma taught me the trick to making every meal taste better. Can I trust you enough to keep her secret?"

She nodded, laughing, and scooted closer, her body inches away from his. He swallowed, and the lump in his throat became a swell that travelled all the way down his body.

"The secret is..." He paused, forcing her to tilt close enough that he could feel soft laps on his skin from her breath and make stray hairs fall across her eyes. "Always have some onions and garlic simmering nearby, even if you aren't going to use them in the dish."

"What?" Her laugh was explosive, and it echoed throughout the big room as she fell back away from him. "You're kidding, right?"

"Nope. Look over there." He pointed to a small pan on the far burner. "Just a little bit, not too much. People smell the onions and garlic, and they automatically think something amazing is cooking. It's subconscious. Worked on you. Think about the reaction you had walking in here."

She chuckled. "That's a pretty good trick, actually. I'll have to use it at my next dinner party."

He enjoyed listening to her laugh. With each day that passed, she became more relaxed, and the intensity of her laugh was a good indicator of how content she was. He was happy to see the carefree woman she could be. And that she was getting more comfortable around him as the days wore on.

He flipped two omelets onto plates and poured tall glasses of orange juice. He put everything onto a large mirrored tray and carried it over to a breakfast nook nestled into a corner of windows.

"Come join me." He slid down the plush bench and patted the space next to him.

She bit her lip as she strolled over and scooted onto the bench. He purposefully left her only a little bit of room and watched her blush as their legs touched under the table. The heat was contagious, and a matching flush flew up the back of his neck.

While they ate, they chatted about various topics. He told her more about his family, and she talked about her cousins. They had more in common than they had previously thought. Both came from complicated families, where the people in each generation stuck together. The plates were empty for a long time before either admitted that the meal was over.

"Thanks for the food." She smiled. "I really needed that. I feel a lot better."

"No problem." He paused, unsure of whether to broach the topic of their budding romance. It was all he could think about, but he didn't know if the same was true for her. Her physical desire was obvious, but she hid her true feelings well. It was possible she thought of him as only a friend with benefits. Well, an employer with benefits, actually.

He finally decided it was best to jump right in and get to the point.

"So…last night, huh?"

He winced at his awkwardness. It was not the

flawless transition into a meaningful talk he had envisioned in his head. The conversation had been flowing so naturally, and now he was tripping over his words, sounding more like a sixteen-year-old after his first date than a thirty-something successful man. He had never been good at the emotional side of dating.

Her lips were pursed, but a giggle burst through.

He slumped down and threw his hands up. She could laugh at him; that was fine. "I'm smooth, I know."

He wanted to talk to her about what had happened between them the night before and what happened to him every time they spoke. He wanted to tell her he was falling for her, but he didn't know how she'd react. So instead of talking, he did what every inch of his body was pushing him to do. He let his actions speak for him.

"How's this for smooth, then?" He leaned forward and caught her mouth mid-laugh with an earnest kiss.

She gasped and sat back. "What about Rose? All the drama at dinner?" She looked at her fingernails. "I understand if last night was a one-time thing since you've got so much going on. I'm really okay with that."

He thought about it. On the one hand, he was trying his best not to rush into a serious romantic relationship, but on the other hand, he truly believed his standing with Rose was slowly improving as time went on. He needed to be able to pursue his own passions while also being a father. There had to be a balance somewhere.

"I think she and I are going to be fine. It will take some work, but I'm willing to put in the time." He had to stop himself from adding, "With both of you." He was falling for her, but he didn't want to scare her away by telling her. Instead, he settled for more flirting. "And you're wrong, you know."

"About what?"

"It couldn't be just a one-time thing. Remember the night of the party? It's got to be a two-time thing, at least." He laughed as her mouth fell open. "You're in deep already."

She was silent for a moment and then just nodded. "I'll do the dishes. You should kick your feet up and relax. It was nice enough that you made food for me."

She piled the plates back on the tray and stood up but immediately sat back down, steadying herself on the table.

"Are you okay?" he asked, quickly running around the table and kneeling in front of her. He put the back of his hand to her forehead to check for a high temperature, but she felt normal. "You're obviously coming down with something. You need to rest."

"I'm fine," she insisted, although her eyes were still closed and her face was pale. "Just give me a minute."

"That's it. I'm going to take care of you, no further discussion allowed." He gently caressed her cheek, and she leaned into his hand in response. His hand trailed down her arm until it met hers, and he tenderly pulled her off the bench. "I'm taking you to the bedroom."

At that, she stopped and looked at him, a small smile creeping onto her face. Apparently, she wasn't feeling too badly. Last night must have been as good for her as it had been for him if she was thinking about that now when she was sick.

"Not for that," he scolded, "although I'm game if

you are." He squeezed her hand. "I'm just going to pamper you a little."

****

Elana had to confess she felt more like herself the longer Bennett held her hand. It had been a long time since a man took care of her when she wasn't feeling well. After years of independence and putting romance on the sidelines in favor of work, she wasn't sure if she even knew how to let someone look after her.

She clasped his hand back in response, ready to let him play nurse, but then she remembered why she was sick. She tensed up and slipped her hand out of his.

"You're sweet, but I promise I'll feel better soon. Like I said, I get like this sometimes. It comes and goes."

She hoped he would take her explanation at face value and not pry for more information. She was close to being ready to tell him about the pregnancy, but couldn't yet. She needed to hide it for a little longer until things were more settled with Rose. She didn't want to guilt him into parenthood, and she knew that if she told him right now, in the middle of his complicated drama, he would be all but forced into it. No, she had to wait until they could both think more clearly. She had to pretend this was just low blood sugar or a stomach bug.

"That's good to hear, but it doesn't change anything. I said no more discussion, remember?" He shrugged and kept walking. "I promise I won't bite. Just a little foot rub to help you unwind. I can't leave you feeling sick after last night. We'll relax for a couple hours and then go back to the house together to talk to Rose."

She was torn, but her body kept moving forward, following him as if he exerted an invisible force that pulled her toward him.

"I guess I can go along with that." She let herself be led to the bedroom, which was half hidden behind a large sliding barn door attached to the wall with industrial wheels. His biceps flexed as he slid the gigantic frame aside to reveal yet another sophisticated room. A small tufted chair sat in the corner, and the only embellishment in the room was an enormous cast iron bed frame that surrounded the bed in a geometric cube, highlighting the clean white bedding. It was a minimalist's dream. Bennett walked over to a polished white dresser, searching for something.

"I know there's lotion in here somewhere," he murmured. "I just need to...aha!" The proud, goofy grin plastered on his face as he displayed a small bottle reminded her of a five-year-old holding up a nest of scribbles on construction paper and begging for it to be hung on the fridge. His innocent excitement was endearing.

"Now go sit down on the bed and take off your shoes," he commanded her in a low voice. "I'm going to pamper you with a foot massage while you get some much-needed rest."

"I'll sit down, but I have to warn you about something." She trailed off as she debated turning down his offer. Her feet were a source of self-consciousness, and she had never before let someone she was intimate with touch her feet.

"What?"

"I have dancer's feet." She paused in expectation and looked at him with apologetic eyes for full effect.

"I suspected. You're a dancer." He replied uncertainly. And then, noticing her grim face, he added, "Is that supposed to mean something to me?"

"It means my feet are gross." Elana winced at the words. "And that's putting it lightly. I work all day on my feet, literally standing on the tops of my toes with my feet stuffed into tight ballet shoes. I put pressure on them in ways no normal person does. They're beat up. I understand if you don't want to touch them. I'm not even sure I want a foot rub."

She was staring at the plush white carpet, watching her feet stroke the threads, when his loud laugh startled her.

"Is that all?" He gasped. "Everyone has gross feet. It doesn't matter, I assure you." He picked her up lightly and slung her onto the bed. Before she had a chance to think, he was slipping her shoes off and casting them to the floor.

"Besides"—he winked—"feet aren't my thing. I want to make you feel good, and giving you a foot massage will do just that. But don't worry, even dancer's feet couldn't turn me off when I'm with you."

Blood rushed into her cheeks. She wasn't sure if it was from the thrill of being swept onto a bed or from embarrassment, but she decided to leave her feet in his hands. He had called her out. She didn't want him to stop being attracted to her. Luckily, the hungry look on his face confirmed that he wasn't bothered by her feet at all.

"Okay," she answered simply.

She closed her eyes and leaned into the mountain of pillows behind her as his hands slowly circled the arch of her foot. With each loop of his strong fingers, she fell deeper into the cushions.

As the initial layer of tension wore off, a pleasant buzz flowed up her leg every time his fingers touched a certain spot. He traced around the perimeter of her ankle, lulling her body into a sense of complacency and comfort before diving in toward the tender spot under the ball of her foot. The waves shooting up her leg were creeping farther north with each rotation of his fingers, and she squirmed at their nearness to her center. She pulled her foot away with a laugh.

"Thank you for the foot rub," she mumbled, not wanting to meet his eyes. "I think I may have been enjoying it too much."

"No such thing," he growled back, his deep tone nothing but serious. He gently pulled her face to meet his. "Are you feeling better? I can keep going if you like."

His emerald eyes bored into hers, forcing the butterflies in her stomach to calm. Time slowed as they stared at each other, and any lingering dizziness disappeared completely. She felt the magnetism of his body as she fought to sit still. They both started breathing more rapidly at the strain.

"Keep going, then," she whispered.

Without breaking eye contact, Bennett reached down and lightly trailed his fingers around the spots on her foot he had just been massaging, immediately setting her nerves on fire again as her body remembered his touch. He quickly identified which spot was driving her crazy and focused his energy there.

She started to relax and lay back, but he clicked his tongue and shook his head at her, bringing her attention back to him. She watched his hand leave her foot and start to travel up the inside of her calf, toward her thigh and beyond. He continued massaging, alternating between light and deep touches to keep her off balance.

She flexed her hands, trying to master the chills that flew throughout her body as his hands continued their expedition at a maddeningly slow pace. She had to do something as an outlet for the electricity. She focused her eyes back into his and smiled mysteriously. She enjoyed seeing him pause for a moment to question her meaning.

****

Bennett watched her stretch her arm out and feel for his leg. She mimicked his actions, tracing a slow, winding path up between his legs and massaging with varying levels of intensity. His inner thighs weren't used to getting attention, and the touch sent almost unbearable tingles up into his groin and chest.

A sigh escaped, and his legs shivered as he battled the urge to pull away. Elana obviously enjoyed exerting her power over him, and he had to admit, the dominance radiating from her eyes had him impossibly turned on. He liked this side of her and was more than willing to let her explore him in ways he hadn't experienced before.

She continued to mirror his movements, as they both teased each other by trailing their hands as closely as possible to their most sensitive areas before narrowly diverting. Each near-miss filled the air with more voltage and anticipation, and his body stood on high alert.

The distinction between his body and hers blurred as he cupped her breasts and she caressed the outline of his abs.

Just when he thought he knew which part she'd touch next, savoring the pattern her hands had fallen into, she suddenly veered off in an unexpected direction and seized his package. Her unpredictable movement nearly sent him over the edge. It was the moment he had been longing for, but he hadn't expected it then. Fireworks exploded, forcing him to double over.

"You got me there." He laughed, picking her up once again and tossing her to the other side of the bed. He'd take the opportunity to challenge her. "My turn now."

She braced herself as he dove toward her, licking the trail his fingers had so recently blazed, until his mouth settled over her center. He nestled in as his arms encircled her legs, holding her steady to him as she squirmed. Her back arched, and his blood boiled as she experienced her final shudders.

It was too much. He had been disciplined while he tasted her, employing his movements with intense precision, but now he could no longer hold back. He loosened his grip on her legs, allowing his arms to slide from her hips to the back of her knees. He still had her in his grasp, and with one thrust, he slid into her.

****

Elana gasped as he filled her, the space between her thighs still pulsating from the first orgasm. Her legs automatically clenched his back, wrapping themselves around him so she could bring him closer with each thrust.

He began slowly, allowing her to feel his entire length, and she was grateful for the long buildup. They rocked together, breathing in harmony and letting out small moans of satisfaction. But soon, the teasing he had started became unbearable.

As if Bennett could read her mind, his gentle strokes turned into more forceful thrusts until they were ravaging each other.

She could no longer stifle her passion. They came together in an overpowering crescendo, and he sank into her with his full weight. It took a moment for him to catch his breath enough to roll over.

"Do you feel better?" he asked with a slight smile.

"I do," she had to admit. "I really do." She rubbed her hand across his cheek before she closed her eyes and fell into a deep sleep.

Chapter 10

Bennett heard the telltale chirp of his phone echo softly from the kitchen. He looked at Elana sleeping on his chest and debated whether he'd be able to slip out from under her arm without waking her. She had fallen deeply asleep after their lovemaking, but his mind and body were still buzzing too much for him to turn them off.

He rocked sideways, planning to slip out the side of the bed without waking her, but the subtle movement was enough to make her sigh and roll away from him. He sat up and gingerly stepped onto the carpet, grateful the text had provided an excuse to get up and move around.

He grabbed his clothes off the floor and headed down the hall, hopping on one foot to get his pants legs on. When he reached the counter, he picked up his phone and looked at the message.

Come home, Dad. Please.

He had only put one arm into his shirt, but he quickly slipped it over his head and checked the text again. Rose was asking him to come home. Something must be wrong.

This was the first time his daughter had ever asked him to join her. It should have been a happy moment, a sign they were becoming closer, but he and Rose hadn't left things in a very good spot last night after their fight over her fake dinner. Given that, the text sounded more ominous than cheerful. Once he added in her recent pattern of acting out, he was worried about why she was asking him to come home.

He wasn't sure he had the parental instinct yet, but all kinds of alarm bells were clanging in his head. He was so nervous that he grabbed his keys and ran out the door without thinking about Elana sleeping in the bedroom next door.

"It's probably nothing," he whispered to himself, "just a teenager being stereotypically concise and her father reading too much into it."

The scenery that had so recently provided a stunning backdrop to a beautiful day flew by unheeded. He had tunnel vision, spending all his energy trying to force negative thoughts out of his head and driving the few minutes from the guest house to the main house through sheer muscle memory.

The car kicked up a cloud of dust as it slowed to a stop in front of the house. He shut off the engine but froze instead of getting out. He had raced home, but now that he had arrived, he suddenly dreaded getting out of the car. Parenting was serious business, and he felt like he was tripping from one crisis to another with Rose. Maybe he was the reason she was spiraling more out of control instead of healing. How would he ever be sure if he was doing the right thing?

He wiped the sweat off his brow for a third time. The car had quickly become stifling in the afternoon sun. It was time to get out. Plus, he needed to see Rose as soon as possible, to show her that he would always come when she called, no matter what. He was dreading the conversation they would have, but he was ready to clear the air after their fight.

His mind suddenly flashed to Elana fast asleep in the clean white sheets of the guest house. He was sure she would stay asleep for a few more hours, maybe even through the night. She had passed out completely after their hour of passion. He hoped to have a heart to heart with Rose and be back at her side before she woke up.

He tried not to think about what would happen if Elana did wake up before he got back, though he knew she'd be mad. After all, there were only so many times a guy could leave a woman after sex before he got sent to the doghouse. He had already left after their one-night stand, and then he ran away after their encounter in the pool. How many more chances would she give him?

Regardless of what would happen with her, he needed to focus on Rose right now. Pushing thoughts of Elana out of his mind, he forced himself out of the car. He strode to the entryway, feigning the confidence he desperately wanted and trying to hold out the hope that Rose was planning some sort of father-daughter bonding.

As he took out his keys to open the door, he was surprised to find it already unlocked. The housekeeper never left the door open. She had learned early on that his father wouldn't tolerate lax security. He pushed the door ajar and leaned his head in, unsure of what he would find.

****

"When did we open a window?" Elana asked idly, enjoying the cool afternoon breeze on her exposed back without opening her eyes. The post-lunch activities had been exhausting, and she had fallen into the deepest nap of her life afterward. She should get up, or at the very least, open her eyes and roll over, but the relaxation of her muscles was too complete. She sighed and gave in. It was settled—she'd have to lie there forever.

She let herself relive the passion she and Bennett had shared earlier. Her body was a map, with lines permanently etched where his fingers had traced and markers at every site he had stopped to conquer. He would be a part of her forever.

She thought about the rest of the day. He wanted to talk to Rose to make sure she was okay. That would be a tough conversation, but it was necessary. Rose might not be happy about their romance at first, and she might even get angrier, but in the long run, openness and honesty were the best policy.

Gently, her fingers began to twitch. She longed to reach out and feel Bennett's skin, to have him caress her. She let her hand slide between the silk sheets in search of his form but instead felt nothing. The silence that had followed her question morphed from comfortable to worrying. Her eyes shot open.

He wasn't there; his side of the bed was empty. For a moment, she couldn't breathe. He had to be somewhere. But the only movement in the room was the fluttering of a curtain in the open window.

She listened for any sign of movement in the house, scanning the dresser and side tables for a note. But when nothing appeared, she hopped out of bed and headed to the open living area. No note was waiting for her there, either. She went from room to room, becoming more frantic with each empty space, but still not wanting to believe he had actually left her. She had to give him the benefit of the doubt. He deserved it...didn't he?

Finally, she headed toward the window to check for his car. When she saw only a black sedan and not the loud yellow sports car they had come in together, the realization hit her: he had left after they had sex. Again.

Rationally, she knew Bennett hadn't really abandoned her after their one-night stand. He had merely treated her like the casual fling she was. But that didn't erase the sting from waking up without the man who had fallen asleep next to her. Now, her feelings for him were intensifying, and the injuries he could inflict on her were growing in magnitude as well.

Why did she keep doing this to herself? He was showing who he was, but she was refusing to believe it. He was a charming man who drew her in, got what he wanted from her, and left. She was getting emotional whiplash going from their amazing time spent together to his continual let downs. Regardless of how intense the connection was when they were near each other, this pattern couldn't continue. She had too much self-respect to keep putting herself in a situation where he would leave her.

The tears pushing their way out blurred her vision as she rushed around grabbing her things. She wanted to get out of there. Not just the guest house, but the entire Wakefield estate. She obviously couldn't control herself when they were together, so she needed to leave. He wasn't good for her, and she should be taking care of herself and the baby right now.

Thoughts of the baby stopped her in her tracks. He was the father; he deserved to know. She couldn't bear the thought of not telling him and putting him through finding out about a secret child again. Once in his life was enough, even if he was a jerk.

At the same time, telling him now seemed impossible. She would have to take some time to distance herself emotionally before she could talk to him rationally about co-parenting. She vowed to tell him in a few months, when the pregnancy was farther along and after she had time to think reasonably.

Elana gingerly picked her bra off the floor. One strap hung loose, a casualty of their night of passion. She still felt the hunger that had led him to so forcefully undress her and for her to not care. She heaved a sigh and tied the strap back together so it would hold for now. The bra was another sign of their doomed relationship.

Once she was fully dressed, she headed out to the sedan in the driveway. She had learned enough about Bennett's family arrangements to know there would be a key hidden somewhere in the car. She would drive back to the house, pack up, and head back to her apartment in DC. If he was at the house, she'd tell him she was leaving, but if not, she could call him from home. The farther apart they were, the easier it would be to talk to him. She would tell him about the baby in a few months, once things had cooled off between them and he had repaired his relationship with Rose. It had to be that way.

But Elana couldn't stop thinking about Rose. She had been through so much in her life already, and leaving could have a ripple effect beyond Bennett to make Rose collateral damage. She was just a teacher to Rose at this point, but she didn't want to taint their friendship. Her baby would be Rose's sibling, and so they would be family, regardless of the type of relationship she and Bennett had. She would need to talk to Rose separately and explain that her sudden departure didn't have to do with her. Maybe her absence would allow Bennett to fix things with Rose more easily.

She was confident in her new plan, although she dreaded it. She would have to psyche herself up to follow through and leave. No matter how many times her brain told her he was bad for her right now, her body still longed for him. She hoped he wouldn't be home when she left so she could talk to him over the phone and explain her sudden departure without the magnetic pull of his physical presence confusing her.

****

"Hello?" Bennett called into the empty foyer, unsure of whether he was supposed to run and call the police about the unlocked front door or go examine every room for an intruder. "If someone is in here, please come out!"

The politeness of the request made him wince. He could never muster a very commanding presence. It was one of the many reasons why his older brother had been their father's favorite.

Determined to appear bolder, he swung the heavy door open and marched loudly in, slamming everything he could grab and knocking against end tables until they shook. Hopefully the noise would deter any potential assailants.

He stomped down the hallway, leaving a trail of echoes in his wake, until he overheard two voices talking in the kitchen. He could barely make out what they were saying, but the familiarity of the second voice sent a cold shiver down his spine. It had been years since he had heard that voice, and he thought it was one he would never hear again.

His body propelled him forward, even as his mind screamed at him to stop. He lunged at the kitchen entry, swinging the door open with a loud creak. The stares of the two women sitting at the counter stopped him dead in his tracks.

Rose and her mother sat across from each other at the table, sipping coffee as if it were the most natural thing in the world.

Chapter 11

"What's your problem, Dad? You sound like you're auditioning to be the next Incredible Hulk. We could hear you from across the house."

Rose sat in front of a mess of crumbs, drinking coffee and eating a croissant without a plate while her mother looked on. She appeared completely unaware of the strangeness of the situation, but Bennett felt like he had entered a parallel universe—one where he was the butt of a giant cosmic joke.

"What are you doing here, Quinn?" he began, practically spitting his words and speaking directly to Rose's mother. "You leave her on my doorstep with no warning after all those years and then have the nerve to show up here?"

"Dad, it's not like that…" Rose started, rolling her eyes and sighing.

"Rose, please go upstairs," he interrupted sternly, still not looking at her and staring daggers at Quinn.

"Dad, I…"

"Please," he begged, quietly this time, straining against the impulse to yell coursing through his body. Quinn had put him in an impossible situation, and she was the reason Rose thought he had abandoned her. For that, she deserved all of his wrath and more. But he had to keep his temper in check in front of his daughter. After all, Quinn was still her mother, no matter what she had done. He couldn't bear for Rose to watch him tear her down. That would make him a monster in her eyes.

Bennett cracked a few knuckles as a release. He needed Rose to leave soon, because he couldn't hold in his true feelings much longer.

"You don't have to be so rude. It's my mom. I asked her to come here and she came. Just like I asked you to come," Rose continued, chattering on and ignoring his obvious discomfort. "I know she wants me back. So I thought you two could work it out. If you give it a try, you might see. If not, she could just take me. I could go home with her today."

He finally turned in Rose's direction, stunned. He didn't understand how she could think her mother would take her home. He was about to ask, but then the answer dawned on him, and the root of all her frustrations became obvious. Her perpetual anger toward him was due to more than believing he had abandoned her. Rose didn't realize why she was living at his house. She didn't know her mother had sent her here, essentially deserting her. In some strange way, Rose thought her mother was blameless.

He didn't know where to begin or even how much of the truth of her history Rose knew. All of the tantrums and fighting of the past few months snapped into much clearer focus when studied through this new lens. Rose thought of Bennett not only as a father who'd abandoned her, but also as a stranger taking her away from her mother. In her mind, he truly was the villain in her story.

He glanced at Quinn who was tracing patterns in the marble countertop. Something seemed off about her. She wasn't following their conversation and didn't appear emotionally invested at all. Her mannerisms were reminiscent of some of his seedier friends from a brief period after college that he preferred not to remember. The way she swayed slightly in her chair and stared through vacant eyes made his stomach turn as he realized she was high.

He forced his attention back to Rose. She was his daughter, and he needed to protect her first. Even if that made her hate him.

"Rose, I know you want to believe your mother and I could get back together, but please, honey, I need you to leave so we can talk. We need to figure things out."

"Fine," Rose declared, looking more like a dejected ten-year-old than a sixteen-year-old. "I don't even care, anyway. I'll be gone from here soon enough, and you won't have to deal with me anymore."

The words stung, but before Rose could leave, they all heard footsteps in the hall. Bennett's heart sank as he recognized Elana's smooth gait. How could he have been stupid enough to leave her at the guest house? Of course she was going to wake up before he had a chance to come back. She was probably furious with him, and now she was going to walk in on this bomb waiting to explode. It was the worst possible time for her to show up. He would have to put her off and deal with the consequences later. He just hoped those repercussions wouldn't cause too much of a problem for their budding relationship.

He steeled himself for a battle on all fronts as Elana slowly pushed the door open and peeked her head around the corner.

****

The kitchen, which had so recently amplified Bennett and Rose's strained voices, was now eerily quiet. The silence hung heavy, expectant. It made Elana nervous to walk in. She pushed the door open slowly, flinching at the creak of the hinge.

Bennett stood in the middle of the kitchen, with Rose and another woman sitting at the table. None of their faces matched. Bennett looked tense and grim, while Rose had a smug grin as she looked from Elana to the woman sitting across from her. Meanwhile, the woman appeared to be lost in other thoughts. She didn't seem to be aware that Elana had entered the room.

"Sorry to interrupt you guys," she stammered, not making eye contact with anyone. She hadn't expected an audience when she headed here from the guest house intent on going back to DC. "I need to speak with Bennett quickly, if that's possible."

Rose came alive at her presence, but her frenzied energy only made Elana worried. Her eyes shone with the same hunger for conflict she had displayed after the botched dinner. She was on the hunt for trouble.

"Not right now, Elana," she practically cooed. "My dad is talking to my mom. Look." Rose stressed the word mom and made a sweeping gesture toward the silent woman, as if introducing her on the stage.

At the word mom, Elana's heart stopped. Her vision narrowed, and the edges blurred as she followed Rose's gaze over to the counter where her mother was sitting. She had to steady herself against the refrigerator to keep her knees from giving out.

Bennett sucked on his teeth and moved toward her as she leaned on the fridge, but she waved him away.

She didn't want him to touch her right now. Her body had a visceral reaction to Rose's words, responding before her mind could catch up, and one touch from him would send her flying out of the room.

Her mind raced to understand this new information. Rose's mom was supposed to be dead. Wasn't that what both Rose and Bennett had told her? Had they been lying to her this whole time? The thought of that level of deception made her sick. They hadn't lied about something small; they had lied about a major aspect of their lives, about someone being dead. They had manipulated her emotions and sense of compassion.

"Your mom?" she gasped, trying to regain her footing. "I thought she was…" She trailed off, not sure what to say. Rose's mother was clearly not dead.

"She *was* gone," Bennett chimed in, his tone hardened. "Apparently she's here now. This was all Rose's doing. She invited her here." He must have seen the pleading confusion in her eyes because he added, "I'm as confused as you. I didn't know she was coming here. I wouldn't have…"

He stopped himself mid-sentence and turned away so Elana couldn't see his face. Wouldn't have what? Lied so blatantly if he knew he would get caught? Slept with her? Or led her on by telling her he cared about her just this morning?

Rose's mom was alive. They had lied to her about that. If they both had lied about something so big, how else had they deceived her? Was Bennett's entire story about not knowing he had a daughter made up, too? All this time, she had thought she might be able to find a place in this family and help mend fences, but she was actually the woman standing in everyone's way. Nobody respected or cared for her at all if they both thought it was okay to lie.

She stumbled to the breakfast nook across from the fridge to sit down. She didn't trust her legs under her at the moment.

"Maybe my mom and dad can get back together," Rose chimed in, sweetly, seemingly oblivious to the discomfort of everyone else in the room.

Her words pierced through to Elana's heart to deliver a final blow. Not only was Rose's mom alive and sitting in the kitchen, there was a possibility for reconciliation. She looked to Bennett for help in deciphering this new information, but he had walked over to the window and now stood with his back to her, gripping the windowsill so tightly his knuckles were turning white. He gave her nothing.

Elana closed her eyes and took a moment to regain her composure and focus. She had come back to the house intending to quit her position and leave, so that is what she would do. This new set of betrayals didn't change anything in terms of her immediate plans, but it did kill her misguided hope that she and Bennett might be able to have some sort of positive relationship as co-parents to their child. Since she couldn't trust him, she would need to rethink his involvement in their child's life. Would she allow a liar to be her child's father?

She forced herself to ignore the situation and quickly repeated the speech she had practiced on her way back from the guest house.

"Well, I just came to tell you that I have to leave. I can't stay here anymore. I'm going to go pack up my things, and I'll contact you from DC to finalize the end of my contract. Sorry for the trouble."

She stood up quietly, waiting for any protests that might indicate her departure mattered, but none came. The silence was deafening. She had at least expected Bennett to question her reasons.

As she walked toward the door, she glanced at him. She could now see his profile, illuminated on one side from the window, and she studied it for any hint of a reaction. Nothing. His perfectly chiseled features had frozen into a statue. She took his mute response as an acceptance of her resignation. If she stayed there and talked for much longer, she wouldn't be able to hold back the tears threatening to escape.

"Bye." Rose waved without a hint of emotion. How could she be so cold after the weeks they had spent working together?

Elana didn't understand how in the span of a few moments her sense of the world could be completely upended. Nothing made sense.

"I—" Bennett started.

"Bye," Elana whispered, cutting him off as she rushed out. She used the rest of her strength to force herself not to look back.

The hallways that were once so beautiful and elegant became oppressive as she ran for the safety of her room. The never-ending procession of family photographs and portraits reinforced how little she actually knew about Bennett, the man she had allowed herself to imagine a future with. It was silly, really. He was nothing but a fling she had naively believed could be more. She should have known sometimes she really could judge a book by its cover.

Packing was difficult through the onslaught of

uncontrollable tears. She texted her mom a short, mysterious message—*Be home soon. Love you.*—that she knew would soon lead to a worried phone call. But she didn't have the energy to explain anything to her mom right now. She turned her phone off and stuffed it into the bottom of her backpack. Her primary focus was leaving the mansion and getting back to DC where she could tend to her wounds and clear her head. She'd figure out what to do after that later.

Logically, she knew she would be okay. She could co-parent with a jerk. Hell, she could even make it as a single parent if she had to. But her emotional side was wrecked. In that moment she realized how deeply she had come to care for both Bennett and Rose. She had built them up as a family—her family—in her mind, and she was mourning the loss of that possibility.

With a final swipe at her tears and a zip of her suitcase, she stood up to leave the room where so many turning points in her life had occurred. In this room she had learned she would be a mother, she had nurtured a growing fondness for Bennett, and she realized her destiny was to live without him. The finality of everything hit her as she turned to go.

Chapter 12

"Rose, please go upstairs. I need to talk to your mother."

Bennett's head was spinning, and he was grasping for a place to begin to fix his life. Just hours earlier he'd had amazing sex with a woman he was falling for and starting to see a future with. Now, she was walking away, and he had stood by silently while her heart was broken. He couldn't correct Rose's misguided statements that he would be getting together with Quinn, not while she was in the room. His primary mission was still to protect his daughter's feelings, even if that meant letting Elana leave devastated and destroying their relationship in one fell swoop. It had taken everything he had to let her crumble and leave without intervening.

Now he needed to address that his daughter was sitting with the mother who had abandoned her, asking for a happy ending for their family. He wanted a happy ending, too, but it wasn't possible with Quinn. How could everything have fallen apart so suddenly?

"I need to talk to your mother," he whispered again, hoping Rose could sense the urgency in his voice. "I don't know why you're acting like this, being rude to Elana when all she's done is help you. And I can't pretend to know why you think your mother and I will get back together. We haven't spoken in sixteen years."

Rose shrank in her chair with each of his statements. Her eyes darted between him and Quinn, still tracing patterns on the marble, and a pang of guilt stabbed him in the chest. This wasn't Rose's fault. Even at sixteen, she was still a child. He couldn't blame her for holding on to the innocent hope that her parents would get back together. That was every child's dream family, especially for a kid who had grown up with a single mother.

He walked over to Rose and placed his hand on her shoulder. "Don't worry," he said. "I'm not mad at you. I just need to straighten things out with your mother first so we can answer your questions. We'll talk about everything later, and you can ask me anything you want. I promise. Please just go to your room for a bit."

Rose opened her mouth as if she had something to say but then slammed it shut. She cracked her knuckles before looking at him and nodding a quick assent.

He watched her slink out of the room. Where had the self-assured young woman he had gotten to know over the past few months gone? Rose wavered between personalities as often as he changed clothes, which was normal for a teenager, he supposed. Especially one going through major life changes. He couldn't imagine what was going through her mind.

Once he no longer heard Rose's muffled footsteps in the hall, he turned to face Quinn and steeled himself for the conversation ahead.

"Why are you here?" he asked, keeping his voice as even as possible. He wanted to give her a chance to explain herself now, before he exploded. He might not have the self-control to listen later.

"Rose called me. I thought things weren't working out with you two, so I came." She shrugged, her eyes roving around the kitchen. "Nice house. Big. I had forgotten how rich you are."

He pushed both palms firmly into the marble, needing an outlet for the anger building in his body. The cool hardness of the counter provided some relief to his heated frame. He'd ignore her attempts to change the subject.

"You sent her here. She had a letter written by a lawyer giving me full parental rights. You relinquished your rights. You shouldn't be here."

She shrugged again, but this time he slammed his hand down on the counter with a loud smack.

"Dammit, Quinn!"

He felt bad when she recoiled at the sound, but he wasn't sure how else to get through to her and make her pay attention. This was a conversation that had to happen. It was months overdue.

"I'm sorry, I'll try to stay calm, but we need to talk about this. Right now."

"Whatever you say."

Her flippant response almost sent him into a tailspin, but he took a deep breath and got himself under control. It was as if she weren't really invested and was only a bystander in the situation with Rose, instead of her mother.

"What were you expecting to do once you got here?" he asked, starting at the beginning. "Based on the documents from your lawyer, I have full legal rights. You gave her up. You have no standing here. I'm her legal guardian now. I'm her father."

He waited, squinting at her face to try and discern

what she was thinking, but her stare was still unreadable.

Lifting one eyebrow, she finally spoke. "I'm not really sure what I wanted to happen when I came here. Didn't think about it." She shrugged. "Rose called, so I came."

"Okay." His words were steady, measured. "But where were you? What happened? I deserve answers. Rose deserves answers. I have been here for months now, trying to be there for our daughter. You left her with no warning. You abandoned her."

"Ugh. Fine, fine," she responded with disgust, raising her hands in mock defeat. "I couldn't do it anymore. Be her mother, I mean. I'm no good at it. I needed to do things for myself for once."

For the first time since entering the kitchen, Bennett took a step back from his outrage and really looked at Quinn. He watched her twitching lips and stilted mannerisms, the constant fiddling. He noted the deep bags under her eyes and lines on her face that surpassed those typical for her age. This didn't fit with his memory of the athletic, always-put-together woman he had known in college. Something had gone wrong in her life. She had made a wrong turn somewhere. She wasn't just high; she was a full-blown addict. It must have been why she gave Rose up.

"Are you high right now?"

"Yeah, so?" she spat, flipping from indifference to abject hatred with no warning.

"So?" he repeated in disbelief. "So this is my house. You sent our daughter here because you didn't want to be a mother. You asked me to be her father and protect her, and then you come here high and expect...what? To be a family? I don't think so."

He was on a roll, blood pumping through his entire body. She had awoken a lion in him, and he was ready to fight for his daughter. He didn't know how long Rose had been exposed to her issues or how difficult it had made her childhood, but it would stop today.

Quinn laughed at his mention of a family. She looked at him like he was crazy. "A family? You think that's why I came here?" She laughed again, a cold, stilted sound that slapped him across the face. "You're as naive as Rose."

She stood and walked around the kitchen, running her hands over the stove and refrigerator. She seemed to be considering her next words carefully.

"Must be easy to judge me, with you living here in this nice, big house. You never needed to work for anything in your life."

He realized what she was after as soon as she mentioned his home for a second time. She wanted money. She only came here to get cash, using Rose's invitation as a way to enter the house and take advantage of her innocence. It was sickening. He had to get her away from Rose as soon as possible.

"You need to get yourself together. Get help." He put his hands on her shoulders and looked her straight in the face. "I need you to hear me and understand me. Get help. After that, you can see Rose again. But until then, I will not let you near her. You won't hurt her any more than you already have. You need to get out now. And you're not getting anything from me, so you can stop looking around the house."

She scoffed, but he continued talking, ignoring her.

"I'll tell Rose you had to go." He gestured for her

to leave.

"Don't be all high and mighty." She sneered at him, but nevertheless turned toward the door. "You were never a father to her."

He couldn't believe what she was saying. How could she stand there and blame him for not being a father? He didn't want to think about what kind of lies she had told Rose about him. Rose grew up being fed stories by Quinn, so her disdain for him made sense. It would take more work than he had imagined to build a relationship with her.

"I never got a chance to be a father." He collapsed on a chair in a pile of tears. "You ruined my life. Not because Rose exists, but because I wasn't there for her. You took that from me when you didn't tell me you were pregnant. I didn't get to see her birth or watch her take her first steps. I missed all the big moments of her childhood. I would have loved her all her life, and you stole that from me."

She rolled her eyes as he sobbed.

"Whatever." She brushed a few crumbs off the counter and onto the floor before walking out the door.

He listened to her retreat and heard the door slam. He sat crumpled, unable to move from exhaustion. He was ready to go to sleep right then and there, but the quiet sound of sniffling out in the hall got his attention. He sat up straight and wiped his face.

"Rose?" he called out, both hoping it was her and praying she hadn't heard this terrible fight. He didn't know how much she knew about Quinn's drug use. Plus, she didn't seem to understand the full extent of her mother's abandonment months earlier. Those were hard truths, and this wasn't the best way to find out, even if they were things she needed to know.

The door once again swung open, and Rose's slack face peeked through the crack. Mascara streaked down her cheeks, and her lipstick was rubbed half off, bleeding outside the lines of her lips. He endured a physical pain at the despair on her face.

"Sit down." He sighed, patting the chair next to him. She looked broken. He didn't want to make things worse, but he would answer all her questions honestly. He just hoped she would let him stay to help pick up the pieces when it was all done.

"Did you hear all that?"

"Mmhmm," she whimpered slowly, gazing down at her fingernails. She picked at a stray piece of dead skin on her thumb.

"Do you have any questions you want to ask? I'm sure that was all confusing." This was his first real parenting trial, and he wanted to do it perfectly. He wanted to take away all her hurt and make sure she felt safe, so he decided to let her take the lead.

"You didn't know about me?" It was barely above a whisper, and he wasn't sure whether it was a question.

He heard the mix of sadness and relief in her voice. He scooped her into a hug, kissed her hair, and whispered back, "No, I didn't. I would have been there."

With those words, they both began to cry. A weight lifted, and he sat a little straighter to support her. They embraced for a long time.

Once her breathing had returned to normal and her body had stopped shaking, she sat back and looked at him.

"I'm sorry you had it so hard. I really am," he said.

"Your mom and I…we aren't going to be together. She has some problems she needs to fix. But if she takes some time to get herself better, puts in the work, she can come back and be a mother to you."

Rose bobbed her head in acknowledgement. "I know you aren't going to be a couple." She scratched the back of her neck. "I always knew that."

He reached out to hug her again but paused when he saw the pained look on her face. Instead, he settled for holding her hand and sitting in silence. She had something to say, and he'd let her say it.

"I know my mom has problems," she said slowly. "She's a drug addict. I thought I came here so she could go to rehab. That's what she told me, at least. I thought this was only temporary and in a few months I'd have my old mom back. There were some good years when I was in elementary school, you know. We had fun. I didn't realize she was done with me."

He had to fight the urge to interrupt and tell her everything would be okay. He settled for squeezing her hand as she continued.

"I was just so mad at you. For everything. I always thought you didn't want me. I thought I wasn't good enough. And then to be left at your house? I just wanted to be anywhere but here. I'm so sorry, Dad."

Bennett's eyes filled as she called him Dad for the first time. "I love you so…" he began, but she stopped him.

"No, wait. I have to finish." Her eyes were filled with determination, and he was impressed at the strong woman he saw in her eyes.

"Go on."

"Okay." She blew out a deep breath. "I'm sorry

because I messed things up for you. I was angry, and so I lied. I lied to Elana, and I sabotaged your relationship. I wanted to hurt you how you hurt me."

"It's no problem, sweetie. We already talked about that fake dinner invitation, and I understand why you invited your mom here. We're fine." She was a kid acting out, and he needed her to know it was okay. They could move on.

"It wasn't just that." Her voice wavered but didn't break. "I told her Mom was dead. I told her you didn't want me and left when I was a kid. I invited Mom here to hurt her. That's why she was so upset when she came in here. It was all my fault!"

For a moment, time stood still. Bennett's face dropped, and a pit formed in his stomach as he thought about each conversation he'd had with Elana over the past few weeks. He remembered her sense of misgiving about him, her quick temper, and her defense of Rose. And then he thought about what he had said in response to her questions. Had he inadvertently confirmed Rose's lies? After their failed dinner date, he had explained he didn't know about his daughter's existence, but did Elana believe him? And he had said Quinn was gone, but did he ever use the word abandoned? He had been so afraid to tell the truth and so vague in his description of how Rose had gotten there that Elana probably thought he had lied about Quinn being dead.

A cold sweat ran down the back of his neck as he fully realized what her perception of him must be. She must think he was a playboy who spit out lie after lie while trying to get in her pants. It would be a Herculean task to get her to see him again, much less to trust him.

As he struggled to grasp that Elana might not ever believe him, he understood the enormity of his feelings for her. He cared deeply for her, and he had told her so, but he had been fooling himself each time he had pretended it wasn't yet love. In facing the prospect of a future without her, he saw he loved her now, in this moment. He had already fallen hard and committed himself to her without realizing it. There was nothing he could do. Their love had been decided the day he walked into the ballet office and back into her life. It was inevitable.

He had to prove to her he wasn't the man Rose had made him out to be. He had to win her back, but he wasn't sure how. Or even when.

His head was cloudy as too many disordered thoughts filled his mind. A light touch on his hand brought him back to the present. He looked down at Rose's hand on his, both so alike in their spindly fingers. He followed the path of her arm up to her frightened eyes. She had been watching him grapple with her revelation, and she looked terrified of his response. He had to put thoughts of Elana aside for now. Rose was the priority.

"Sweetie…" he began, softening as her lips quivered. "I still love you. I do wish you hadn't lied, but I understand. You were hurt and upset. I'm your father, and it's my job to take away your pain. I wasn't doing a good enough job. I'm going to from now on."

"Dad, I'm sorry," she said again, shrugging and shaking her head.

"It's okay. We'll work it out. We'll fix everything together." He hugged her, thinking about how in the world he would go about making the two women in his life feel safe and loved after all the ways they thought he had failed them. It would take a lot of work, and the job wouldn't be complete for a long time, but he was up to the challenge.

Chapter 13

Two Months Later

The grainy black and white photo on the fridge stared out at Elana, catching her attention every time she walked by. The pixels were blurry, and she had to tilt her head to make it out, but she was starting to be able to identify the gummy bear in the ultrasound photo as her future child.

Her mother had accompanied her to the first ultrasound appointment at twelve weeks, right when she got home from Bennett's house. They'd held hands throughout the appointment, her mother so excited about the thought of a grandchild that she neglected to ask any questions about what had happened while she was away. She hadn't even inquired about the father in the beginning, although Elana supposed it was obvious he wasn't currently in the picture. Once the shock and novelty of becoming a grandmother had worn off, though, the questions had begun.

She hadn't known how to respond to her mother's well-meaning curiosity. No, the father didn't know about the baby yet. Yes, she would tell him eventually. No, he didn't live in DC. And they weren't together as a couple, right?

The sting from being asked about their relationship status hadn't diminished over time. Even now, two months after coming home, she still felt a pang in her gut when her mother mentioned his name. She braced herself as she announced her pregnancy to each new friend, anticipating how they would interrogate her about the mystery man who was the baby's father.

But the hardest part of being back home were the dreams. At night, her protective guard came crashing down, and an onslaught of images of Bennett flooded her mind. She never dreamed about his deception or his tendency to leave her after their nights together, and that made it worse. It was much harder to wake up alone after a night spent envisioning the perfect guy than it would be to hold steadfast in her anger if she dreamed about his offenses.

More than once, she had started to dial his number into her phone, but each time, her brain talked her fingers out of it. He had called and texted practically non-stop in the week after she left, but she ignored it all. She'd been too upset, and frankly, too concerned about announcing her pregnancy to her mom and getting her doctor visits in order to worry about him. By the time she'd started to get her life organized, she was determined to not backtrack and dwell on him. Plus, she needed to prepare herself for the upcoming conversation where she'd tell him about the baby. If she went into that meeting with any vulnerabilities, she didn't know what would happen.

She rubbed her hand across the picture on the fridge, trying to fathom how that blurry bean could be a person growing inside her. With each passing day, she became more attached to the idea of being a mother and less daunted by the prospect. With her free hand, she cradled the small bump that seemed to have appeared overnight and tried to feel movement, although it was too early. Her stomach wasn't big, but the bump was noticeable on her slight dancer's frame, and it constantly surprised her. She had dedicated her life to forcing her body to bend to her will in order to achieve perfect form. She still wasn't used to being out of control with how it grew.

She pulled the picture from under the ballet shoe magnet and slid it gently into the pocket on the side of her purse, just as she did every day. More than once, she had tried to leave it at home. After all, there was no reason to bring it with her everywhere—no one really wanted to look at an ultrasound picture, no matter how interested they seemed. But she still wasn't ready to be without it.

Grabbing her keys and purse, she headed out the door. She was on her way to her new job, teaching ballet at a small private school in DC. Her experience with Rose made her want to get more involved with kids, and she was loving it. The students were happy and optimistic, and that feeling rubbed off on her. She hadn't realized just how burned out she was with the world of professional ballet until she took a step back from it.

As she skipped down the stairs into the cold winter day, she had to shield her eyes from the dazzling sun. That momentary blindness was all it took to make her trip over a person sitting at the bottom of the steps. She fell forward, throwing her purse out in front of her and tensing for the inevitable tumble she was about to take. But instead of a hard landing on the concrete, strong arms grabbed her and lifted her back to her feet.

Her eyes were shut tight, but she knew exactly who

had caught her. His smell and embrace were seared into her mind, and she had an instinctual reaction to his touch. She stepped back a beat too late to look natural, pushing away the hands supporting her.

She took a breath and gathered her courage before looking straight into Bennett's emerald eyes.

****

Bennett had been sitting on Elana's frozen stoop for the past forty-five minutes trying to work up the courage to knock. He didn't know what to expect. He had tried to get in touch with her after she left, leaving message after message on her phone, but after a week of complete silence, he decided to take a step back and give her some space.

That time away from romance was just what he needed to get his head in order and start rebuilding the broken pieces of his relationship with Rose. After the blow up with Quinn, both he and Rose were raw with emotion. Every little thing seemed to hit an exposed nerve.

He could see the pain Rose carried in her eyes, and he had to do something for her to heal the wounds of the past. He suggested she revisit the therapist she had written off a few months ago. Rose agreed, surprisingly, but only under the condition that Bennett also begin therapy. And so once a week, they started a routine of heading one town over, having a big pancake brunch at the lone diner, and then trekking off to therapy. While Rose was in her appointment, he wandered through the community gardens at the outskirts of town, purposefully trying to slow down and appreciate the growth of the plants around him. It calmed and centered him before he went in for his appointment.

Therapy was a new experience for him, but it was paying off. He and Rose were able to spend whole days together now without clashing. He even found a way through her angsty teenage facade, getting her to crack big, toothy smiles every now and then. The therapist also confirmed his decision to give Elana some breathing room, pointing out that although he was in love with her, he needed to get his act together before he could truly be there for someone in a romantic relationship.

He looked down at the flushed woman who had just fallen into his arms and was yanked into the past as an intense physical connection flooded his body. When they were apart, Bennett had been able to think objectively about their relationship, but now that he was here, holding her, the urge to be with her became more primal. Something was different about her, too, but he couldn't put his finger on it. She looked radiant. Before he had a chance to speak, she pushed herself up and hopped out of his arms.

"What are you doing here?" she cried a little too loudly, clearly thrown off guard. He watched her hands run through her disheveled hair and smooth her clothes, the motions of a woman who cared whether he found her attractive. That was a good sign at least.

"I came here to talk to you," he said calmly, wanting to make her feel comfortable with him. "After the way things ended at my house, I had to come and tell you the truth. I couldn't leave it like that." And then after a pause he added, "I couldn't leave us like that."

She seemed to consider this, as her furrowed brows revealed an inner struggle between the part of her that wanted to tell him off before walking away and the part of her that wanted to hear him out. He could only hope her curiosity would win out.

"Fine," she relented at last. "But let's go back up to my apartment. It's too chilly out here on the street."

She bent down to pick up the scattered contents of her purse, and he crouched to help.

"Your nose and cheeks are red. How long have you been out here?" she asked, eyeing him suspiciously.

"Just a few minutes," he lied, not wanting her to know if she hadn't come out and tripped over him, he may not have been brave enough to knock on her door for another hour. "I was just…"

Bennett trailed off as he grabbed items spilled from her purse. They were strewn all over, and her back was to him as she collected pens that littered the grass. But his eyes were glued to the black and white photo on the ground in front of him. He recognized it as an ultrasound photo, but why did she have it?

"What is that?" he asked, suddenly unable to catch his breath.

Elana turned, and her eyes followed his to the photo on the ground. They widened for only a moment, but it was long enough for him to identify the fear in her eyes. She grabbed the picture quickly but gently and placed it in her purse. He knew from the tender way she held the ultrasound that it was hers. She was pregnant.

She was looking down and fiddling with her hands. Her lips rubbed together in stilted movements. As his eyes followed her worried movements, he became aware of the slight swell of her belly under her shirt that hadn't been there before. She was definitely pregnant, and based on the time they'd spent together, it had to be his.

He waited in silence for the words that would come, his body humming as he tried to process the news. He was overwhelmed with a kind of fear he had never experienced before. It was anxiety with a twinge of optimism.

She looked so nervous, like a kitten without its mother, but she didn't need to be scared. He had come here to tell her that he loved her, and this wouldn't change his feelings. If anything, it intensified them. Sure, he wasn't expecting to become a father again so soon, and yes, becoming a dad was a scary thought, but the baby itself wasn't. He had already imagined a future with her. This was it.

Finally, after what felt like an eternity, he grabbed her and enveloped her in a tight hug.

His embrace released a valve of emotions, and she began to sob. He was worried for a moment as her body remained slack and she didn't hug him back, but when her arms finally wrapped around his back and her hands grabbed his shirt, he knew she was crying tears of relief. How long had she been keeping this secret? And at what cost? It couldn't have been easy to bear this alone.

****

Elana's cries came in waves, making her whole body shake as she gasped for air. She had been dreading this moment for months, but now that it was here, she was only aware of a lightness, and her body was in a state of shock. The burden of shouldering this life-changing secret alone was gone, regardless of how Bennett responded.

As each tear fell, a little of the stress she had been

carrying dissipated. A comfort replaced the fear and worry that had dominated her life. He hadn't run away screaming at the sight of an ultrasound photo. Instead, he was hugging her. That meant he would be there for the baby in some capacity, although she wasn't sure exactly how yet.

She pushed him away and wiped her cheeks. She still didn't know what to do or how to move forward.

"It's okay," he offered, brushing a loose curl behind her ear. "It's cold out here. Let's go inside. Then we can both say what we need to say."

She nodded. She was grateful he was remaining calm and taking the lead. If he freaked out, then they would both be overwhelmed with emotions. At least this way they could have an open conversation.

Stuffing the last of the fallen items into her purse, she headed back up the stairs. She led him through the narrow hallway and to her door, pausing before putting the key in the lock.

"Before we go in and talk, I just wanted to say that despite everything, some part of me is glad to see you," she admitted. "We have a lot to catch up on, but I needed to say that first, in case you're too mad at me later."

She was worried that keeping the pregnancy a secret would be an unforgivable offense, especially since it had already happened to him once. No matter how badly their romantic relationship had ended, and how angry he had made her, the baby was a separate issue.

"Okay," he replied.

As they walked into the apartment, Elana straightened chairs and folded a blanket thrown haphazardly across the couch. After the magnificence and impressive standard of cleanliness in his mansion, she was embarrassed for him to be in the cramped city apartment she shared with her mother. She quickly grabbed the stray towel from this morning's shower and threw it into her bedroom, shutting the door and turning around. He stood examining a picture on the wall as if pretending not to notice her last-minute clean up.

"Sorry about the mess," she stuttered. "I wasn't expecting any guests."

"Don't worry about it." He walked straight to the faux suede couch and gestured for her to sit down next to him. He waited for her to take off her coat and make her way to the sofa. Once she finally sat down, he began.

"Tell me." He placed his hand on hers while those damned green eyes bored into her. "You can do it. I'm ready."

He already knew about the baby. How could he not after the ultrasound photo and her tears in the street? He was trying to make this easy for her, but it was still difficult to get the words out.

"I'm pregnant," she blurted and then held her breath, waiting for his inevitable outburst.

Chapter 14

"Pregnant." Bennett halted. He pushed his breath out forcefully and looked up at her with a determined stare. "Okay. How are you feeling? What can I do?"

Elana was astonished at his calm, measured response. He wasn't yelling or getting angry. He wasn't accusing her of anything or questioning whether it was his. He was just being supportive, seeing what she needed and what she thought about the baby.

"I don't need anything right now," she stammered, caught off guard. This was not the way she had expected this conversation to go, and she wasn't prepared for it. In fact, she had never been able to think beyond the initial pregnancy announcement. "I just wanted to tell you because you're the father."

He closed his eyes at the word father, and she wasn't sure whether he was happy or upset. She frowned and stared at him, as if that would allow her to read his mind.

"I mean, you can choose your level of involvement, of course. I know things are complicated in your life right now, and this was obviously unexpected, so I'm not going to force you to—"

"Stop," he interrupted, placing his hand on her leg.

The words she had been saying were now caught in her throat.

"I'll be there. There's no doubt about it."

He brought his gaze up to hers, and a tear slowly rolled down his cheek. She smiled at him before realizing tears were also falling down her face, softly this time.

"I missed one kid growing up. Do you really think I'd miss another?"

He was so earnest, and it was more than she could have hoped for. These were the words she hadn't allowed herself to dream about over the past two months. He would co-parent this child with her. Another burden was lifted as one of the questions about her future was answered. This baby would have two loving parents. But what would their relationship be?

As her nervousness subsided, she began to think more clearly. She was happy about his reaction, that was certain, but a darkness was creeping into that joy. She remembered how they had left things at the mansion. She thought about how he had lied to her about Rose's mother, how he had left her after spending the night together, and just simply, how complicated his family life was. That chaos left a shadow on her mood.

She wasn't sure how to approach that mess, or if she even should. After all, he didn't owe her anything. They had never committed to each other. In fact, if she had bothered to analyze his behavior at the time, she had to acknowledge he was just having a fling. And that wasn't a punishable offense. She had never asked for more. His actions had told her what she needed to know, but she didn't listen. It was her own fault she'd fallen for him. He could still be this baby's father without explaining his motives or repairing their relationship. Plenty of people raised children together with a difficult past and without romantic involvement.

"A kid," he breathed out, shaking his head. His words brought her back to the present. "Wow."

A small smile flashed across his face, reigniting the flutter in her heart. He had always been irresistible to her, and now that smile meant more than just a physical attraction. It meant fatherhood.

"Yeah. Sorry to catch you off guard. I kept trying to tell you, and then, you know…" She trailed off, raising her eyebrows and circling her hands to show the story continued.

"Life happened. It got complicated, I know," he finished her sentence for her, exuding a peacefulness that threw her off. Why was he so calm and content about his family situation and their relationship? For most of the time she was at his house, he had been in crisis mode, trying to make things right with Rose. Not to mention the turmoil of her last day there. Why didn't any of that seem to matter to him now?

"Exactly…" she said, her voice rising with the question she was too scared to ask. She wanted to know his take on their fling, but asking about it would reveal more about her feelings than she wanted to.

"Look," he said, squaring his body to her. "I came here today because we need to talk. I have a lot of explaining to do. This baby is a surprise. A wonderful surprise, actually. And one we'll figure out together. But I need to go back to the day you left for a minute."

Hope rose in her chest even as she steeled herself for more lies. She figured he would make up some story about Quinn and Rose just to placate her.

"It's really okay." She shrugged. "You don't owe me an explanation. We don't have to make those weeks into more than they were. It was a fling. That's it. We aren't required to make it more than that just because of a baby."

She didn't believe her own words even as she said them, but she tried to use her most authoritative voice. He seemed to believe them, though. He winced and shook his head, his hands rising.

"You're wrong," he said. "They were more than that to me. You were more than a fling. And I'd be willing to bet I was more than just a fling to you."

His words shook her to her core, although her body remained stock still. It was as if any movement might make him lose his place, take back his admission, and bolt out the door. Over the past months, she had tried to convince herself he didn't matter to her in that way, but her immediate response to his words tore down her facade.

When she didn't say anything, he kept going. "I know you think I lied to you about many things, and I can't imagine how you'd forgive me, but I want you to know I didn't lie. Never."

Holding her breath, Elana's pulse quickened. He had to be just covering up his past behavior, right? Her mind tried to calm her body. She was attempting to think about his words logically, but that seemed impossible.

"Rose was having a hard time, as you know." He paused.

She was finally able to regain control of her muscles enough to tilt her head slightly forward.

"We've been through a lot since you left. We started therapy. Both of us. We try to talk every day, no matter if it's hard or one of us is angry. The point is, we're working hard at being father and daughter. At being happy."

She gave a small smile. That was good news, of course, but it didn't justify or excuse his behavior toward her. It made her hopeful for the years of co-parenting ahead of them, but not for anything else. "I'm really glad for you two."

"Thanks. I mean, I know that's not an explanation. But don't worry, I'm getting to it." Bennett wiped his forehead and readjusted in his seat. He looked as nervous as she had ever seen him.

She tried to soften her face a bit to encourage him but failed when she remembered the pain she'd endured the first few weeks after leaving his mansion.

"Rose told me everything that you two talked about. A lot of it was lies. I don't blame her, of course. She was just a kid in a tough spot. She made up stories to cause trouble because she was so angry at me. She told me she made you believe her mother was dead. She confessed to purposefully lying, and she's really sorry about it."

He stopped to run his hands through his hair while she hung on his every word, silently begging him to continue. This explanation made sense. It aligned with her experiences with Rose.

After a few seconds playing with his hair, he continued, "Considering all the stories she told you, I imagine I must have looked like an ass. I understand why you left. How could you trust me if you thought I was someone who would lie about the mother of his child being dead? It would have been impossible."

He turned to her and scanned her up and down. His face contorted when his gaze landed on her stomach. "And geez! You knew you were pregnant at that time, didn't you?" He looked truly upset. "That must have been terrible!"

She stood up and walked around to the back of the couch, needing a moment to process. She was trying to listen to him but was caught on his statement that Rose had lied about her mother being dead. She already knew Rose had lied, and that was bad of course, but his lie had been the major betrayal. She could have sworn he'd confirmed she was dead. One by one, she tried to replay all her discussions with him. What exactly had he said?

"But you told me she was dead, too. I didn't just think you were a liar. I knew it."

Bennett nodded. "I've gone over that night with the botched dinner so many times, trying to recall our exact conversation, and I know why you'd think that. I said she was gone, which was true, but poor phrasing given the story Rose had made up. I was still embarrassed about the whole situation with Rose and her mother, and I was too vague. It was all a big misunderstanding. You've got to believe me. I never said she was dead. I would never lie to you."

His pleading eyes were clouding her judgement, and she had to turn away again.

She conjured up that night in vivid detail—the embarrassment of being stood up, Rose's confession of lying about dinner so Bennett would look bad, their conversation about his past where he seemed so vulnerable, and then the steamy night spent exploring each other's bodies. She flushed at the image of their bodies entwined on the plush sofa.

She shook her head to clear out that thought. He was telling the truth. He had said Rose's mother was gone. She hadn't pushed for more of an explanation at the time because it supported the story Rose had given. And it would make sense for her to have lied. That fit in with her pattern of destructive behavior. Rose had been so mad at the world and even admitted to lying to try to get between them. His story checked out.

When she turned back to him and saw the strained look on his face, she realized how long she had been silently staring away from him. He looked terrified, like she held his whole world in her hands and might crush it at any moment.

"Well?" he asked quietly, his voice shaking.

"I believe you." She walked over to him and took his hand in hers. After everything they had been through and everything they still had to face, she was ready to trust him and move forward. "It's okay. I believe you."

She went to hug him, but he stopped her.

"There's one more thing I need to tell you."

She examined him, looking for an indication of what this new thing could be, but found no hints. What was the next bomb he'd drop? They had been through everything already; what more could there be?

"I love you."

Time stopped, but Elana responded straight from her heart, before her mind could analyze the decision and talk her out of it. "I love you, too."

Melting into him, she was pulled forward through a force outside herself. His strong arms supported her as they lifted her into a deep kiss that wiped her mind blank. They were one, and that felt perfect.

A warmth washed over her body, leaving her toes tingling. She wanted nothing more than to be in this moment forever.

Epilogue

One Year Later

"Shh! She just went to sleep." Elana gave Bennett a playful jab in the ribs.

"I'll be quiet," he whispered in her ear, nibbling the bottom of her earlobe and hopping away before she could poke him again.

"Hey!" She laughed and sat on the bed, tugging at her raggedy T-shirt and smoothing her unwashed hair.

She hadn't been feeling like herself since Lexie's birth, but she had never looked so beautiful to him. The world had completely changed when Lexie was born, and he had everything he ever wanted.

He walked over and gave her a long, soft kiss on her lips. "Have I told you lately that I love you?"

"Only every day." She smiled.

Despite his sleep-deprived haze from the endless hours of bouncing a crying baby, he felt like the luckiest guy in the world. He and Elana were taking it slow and not living together yet, but this was the happiest he had ever been.

A month after finding out about the baby, he had moved to DC and bought an apartment a few streets over from hers. They had agreed to start out as friends, despite their mutual declarations of love. The attraction was still there of course, but they were focused on Rose and the baby. After a few months, though, their inevitable relationship had taken root. Now, she spent most nights at his apartment. Despite the toll of waking up with Lexie several times a night, they were basking in the bubble of young love. During the day, he stayed busy taking Rose to and from school and exploring his new city with Lexie. It was close to perfect.

Rose had been over the moon to move to the city, as country life was apparently way too slow for a seventeen-year-old. She had jumped at the offer to enroll in a new school and was flourishing there. They were still going to therapy, and things were rocky sometimes, but good days came more often than bad. She had even started visiting her mom every once in a while, after she completed rehab.

"Why don't you lay down for a bit?" he suggested. And then, holding his fingers up like a boy scout, he added, "I promise to be completely silent. Not one of the ladies in this house will be disturbed by me."

"You know what?" She sighed. "I think I will."

He kissed her, watched her lay down on the bed that hadn't been made since before Lexie was born, and then snuck out the door to the living room. He sat down with a book, trying his best to fulfill his promise of silence, but couldn't concentrate on the words. Instead, he went over to his duffel bag and pulled out a diamond ring, twirling it to see the light reflected in each angle. He could imagine a different scene from their future life projected in each side of the perfectly cut diamond.

This was the life he had always wanted, even if he never admitted it to himself. Fate had thrown Elana into his life when he most needed her, and no matter how many obstacles were flung at them, they always returned to each other. If they could weather the past year, then they could make it through anything. He wanted to spend his life with her, and he was sure she felt the same way.

He slid the ring into his pocket and headed for the kitchen. He had been planning to wait for the perfect evening to propose. He wanted to take Elana to the fanciest restaurant in town, and then they'd go out for drinks and dancing. Finally, he'd bring her to a rooftop bar overlooking the Potomac River and get down on one knee under the stars to ask her to marry him. But all of that extravagance seemed unnecessary. He just wanted to have her as his fiancée as soon as possible, so he changed his plans.

Looking at what he had in the kitchen cabinets, he decided to cook a nice meal, do all the laundry, and clean whatever he could before she or Lexie woke up. He could accomplish that quietly. Then he'd surprise her with the biggest question of all. They were already a family, and it was time to make it official.

Fingering the ring in his pocket once again just to make sure it was still there, he whispered, "This is Elana, my wife." He closed his eyes and smiled, letting happiness wash over him at the image of introducing her as his partner. Then, finally, he clapped his hands and looked around the kitchen.

"Get to work," he scolded himself. "Only a few hours left to make everything perfect."

A word about the author...

Riley Blair is a writer of Contemporary Romance who lives in the heart of Virginia wine country with her kids, husband, and bald dog. Before finding her way to romance, she spent a few years writing short stories in as many different genres as possible. When she isn't lost in a work of fiction, you can usually find her getting messy with her kids, playing board games, or singing show tunes too loudly.

~*~

Find Riley online at:
https://twitter.com/the_write_riley

Thank you for purchasing
this publication of The Wild Rose Press, Inc.

For questions or more information
contact us at
info@thewildrosepress.com.

The Wild Rose Press, Inc.
www.thewildrosepress.com

To visit with authors of
The Wild Rose Press, Inc.
join our yahoo loop at
http://groups.yahoo.com/group/thewildrosepress/